SO MUCH
MORE THE MAN

SO MUCH MORE THE MAN

STEPHAN LE MARCHAND

The Book Guild Ltd

First published in Great Britain in 2021 by
The Book Guild Ltd
9 Priory Business Park
Wistow Road, Kibworth
Leicestershire, LE8 0RX
Freephone: 0800 999 2982
www.bookguild.co.uk
Email: info@bookguild.co.uk
Twitter: @bookguild

This work is entirely fictitious and bears no resemblance to any persons living or dead.

Typeset in 12pt Adobe Jenson Pro

Printed on FSC accredited paper
Printed and bound in Great Britain by 4edge Limited

ISBN 978 1913551 971

British Library Cataloguing in Publication Data.
A catalogue record for this book is available from the British Library.

FOR S, S AND E.

1

OCTOBER 2018

WORCESTERSHIRE

She is brutal with the penstemon. It's leggy and she is offended by its appearance. She knows she should have insisted on cutting it back when he had said let it be. The two hollyhocks, brown and stale, are also cut down almost to ground level. She enjoys how sharp the new secateurs are.

The dogs next door are released into the garden, barking pointlessly as they run towards her, only to be stopped by the wire mesh. She wants to attack them as well. She sees the tired geraniums in the blue pot, one of the pots he planted, and deadheads them before changing her mind and pulling them out roughly. She sees the soil on her hand is turning red. Closer inspection reveals a cut, and the blood now starts to run slowly. She is in no pain, but she is annoyed by her inefficiency. She holds her hand under the outside tap and then goes inside to wash her hands and to find a plaster.

Patched up, she checks her watch. She goes upstairs, puts on the jeans that have been lying across the director's chair he once received as a present and takes from her wardrobe the first blouse she sees, plain white cotton. For once she does not look in the mirror on the landing. She snatches the car keys from the bookcase in the hall.

She starts the car and tries to set the satnav, the system something she finds frustratingly counter-intuitive, but she always insists on doing it herself even when he quietly tuts and offers to help. She inhales deeply and deliberately slowly, pauses briefly, and then exhales through slightly parted lips before putting the car in gear and setting off.

Visiting hours start at 2pm and she is confident she will have plenty of time to complete the journey again, to find a parking space and to compose herself before going in.

The first part of her drive is particularly familiar and she starts to breathe more naturally. She has come this way so often with him when the boys had practices and matches in Pershore and sometimes in Evesham. The sky is a cerulean blue and the trees are standing tall, proud of their autumnal brilliance, unaware of the transient nature of their majesty, but she does not notice. She stares at a long stretch of cats' eyes and then at the white lines marking the middle of the road. It is a day to make one thankful, but her face is set, mouth downturned and eyes unblinking. She is rehearsing again the lines she composed during what felt like a sleepless and almost endless night. She is still not used to his not being alongside her, not used to not feeling the heat coming from his body even when their room is freezing cold as the north wind comes in through the ill-fitting Juliet-balcony windows. *Would that vast empty space in their bed ever be filled again?* she wonders.

She sees signs for Bretforton and remembers having a wonderful pub lunch there with him and their dear friend, Tony, who died some fifteen years ago. She can't remember the name of the pub and sees no reason to search her memory, but she can picture its stone floor and massive open fire, and she recalls the three of them going for a lovely long walk to build up an appetite for the hearty lunch the pub served. Poor, poor Tony, the godfather of their two boys, who for ten years had never missed a birthday or any other significant moment in the boys' lives; who had supplied them with so many bits of sports kit and who had been there to witness their achievements, and to console them when things had gone wrong; and whose death had played such an important part in their growing up.

When she sees signs for Honeybourne, she starts to try to remember the names of the other stations between Foregate Street and Oxford. Moreton-in-Marsh, of course, and she remembers him once playing cricket there before they had the boys, and the luxurious picnic they had enjoyed before the match.

She knows from past experience that parking is free but grips the steering wheel more tightly when she sees that the car park looks full, partly because not all of it is in use, some of it closed off for pothole repairs. But she finds a space in between almost identical, offensively bright, red Ford Fiestas, slips into it, turns off the ignition and, despite her set jaw, immediately starts to cry. *I can't do this again. It gets harder every time*, she thinks, but she knows she has to. She searches in her handbag, amongst the ancient receipts, small notebook, brush, comb, lipstick and different pens – what he refers to as 'the detritus' – pulls out a couple of tissues, and, looking in the vanity mirror, dabs the corner of her eyes and briskly and harshly blows her nose. Breathing slowly and deeply, she manages to compose herself a little, and remembers to lift up the vanity mirror flap to stop him tutting. She checks she has her passport, the VO and a £1 coin in her bag, gets out of the car and follows the signs to the 'Visitors Centre', for once not registering the absent apostrophe, wishing she was invisible and shaking her head in disbelief at where she is and what she is doing.

She shows her ID and the visiting order, has her fingerprints taken and then, using the £1 coin, deposits her handbag in a battered and rusty grey locker. Briefly she thinks of the lockers she uses at the gym, their gym, but he hasn't been there with her for weeks. She looks at her fingers and thinks of other occasions when she has had her prints taken: happy ones, when travelling on holidays with him to the United States. Would she ever holiday with him again? Could she bear to holiday on her own? She is escorted with two other visitors to the main prison. Outside the visits hall, a severe-looking female officer with very prominent veins in her arms searches her and then passes over her a metal detector, like the ones she has seen at airports. Also in the room is an Alsatian on a chain lead held by a huge man who looks as though he might once have been a boxer and who now drinks a lot. His hands are swollen, red and calloused. She guesses the dog is there to scent illegal substances and just for a moment has the dreadful thought that maybe someone has planted drugs on her and she will be put in a cell herself. She tries to catch the dog's eye, to assure it she is innocent, but it shows no interest and she is allowed to make her way to the visits hall.

He is already sitting behind a small, plain square table and she is grateful he is the closest prisoner to her. She manages to stifle a gasp when she sees how haggard he looks, and the black rings under his bloodshot eyes. *You can do this. You will do this*, she says to herself. When he sees her, he stands up to hold her should she make any suggestion she wants to be held, but she is already sitting herself down. She doesn't look at him as he resumes his seat, and she thinks he must be trying to anticipate what she is going to say. She is sitting, perfectly still, not looking at him, her face in almost full profile, tilted upwards slightly in what she intends to be a show of defiance.

2

AUGUST 2018

SATURDAY
WORCESTER

Philip arrived at his car, parked on College Green, and was surprised to hear the cathedral clock already chiming eleven. He remembered someone telling him that cathedral bells are the loudest musical instrument in the world, and then he recalled with a smile reading recently that a bell-ringer somewhere had needed to be rescued after he had been flipped upside down and trapped eighty feet up after catching his foot in a rope.

He had been in town for nearly two hours: having a haircut, even though Laura said he didn't need one; buying food at M&S; and looking at but not buying shirts, the latest TVs and more Sonos equipment he didn't need and couldn't afford.

Three more days, he calculated, and he would be exactly halfway through the summer holidays and the new school year would be looming. Retirement was getting closer and he felt happy that he had enjoyed what most people, he hoped, would agree had been a successful teaching career. He was loading the shopping into the boot when he heard a familiar voice.

'Hi, sir. Enjoying your holiday?' He looked up: James, one of his U6 last year, was smiling at him, looking chilled in casual and expensive shirt, shorts and shades.

'Hi, James. Yes, you bet. Better than work, isn't it? Oh, sorry – forgot you don't know what work is. Actually, I take that back: in the last few months you were a character transformed. It's never too late. At least I hope it wasn't for you. We'll find out next Thursday, won't we? Nervous?'

'Quietly confident, actually, sir. About English, anyway. Bit worried about history, though. The European paper was a complete...' He didn't finish his sentence.

'Everyone felt the same, though, didn't they? I really do hope it's a good day for you. No doubt I'll see you – to congratulate you, I hope. It's Warwick, isn't it, that you're hoping to go to?' James nodded. 'Top place. Who'd have thought, eh, a few years ago when you were getting wound up about that GCSE poetry anthology?'

'Oh, God, yes. Heidi with her b... linking blue hair!'

'Such a good poem. Bet you like it now, don't you?'

'Yeah, it's OK. Anyway, sir, I'd best be off. I'm meeting Rich for brunch at Nando's.'

'Say hello to him for me, please. And behave yourselves.'

'As if. See you, sir.'

Philip watched him go for a few seconds, smiling at his confident, springy step, then sat down on a low wall and looked through and beyond the market stalls set up on the Green at the various school buildings surrounding it. All places bringing back happy memories. Mostly. One or two bad episodes – nothing dreadful, but at the time they had still been enough to keep him awake at night. Hundreds of good ones, but it is always the bad ones that linger and which still niggle away years later. Familiar exteriors: he'd walked past them thousands of times and they hadn't changed in thirty-five years, even if the various doors had been painted a number of different shades, heritage colours, of course. He knew the insides so well, the corridors, the nooks and crannies, the dusty cupboards, the posters and displays on the walls, the teaching rooms. His classroom, with his files and books. He knew that they would all have to be moved when he retired. There was no room for any more books at home, Laura had insisted. And what about those files and folders containing a lifetime of preparation and accumulated resources? He would never use them again. What was the point of cluttering up the garage? The files would get damp and mouldy and eventually he'd give in and chuck them in bin liners and take them to the tip. Better to leave them in the department for others to use – for the older hands to see how he had done things and for the younger teachers to see just how much work is done during a full career. Actually, would anyone even look at them? Probably not. *Even so*, he thought, *I can be quietly proud of what I have achieved.*

No reason to go home quite yet, so he thought he'd take a look at the various market stalls displaying their wares on the Green. Lots of over-priced plants. Enormous piles of multi-coloured fudge, being sold by a pink-faced middle-aged couple in matching pink polo shirts whose fibres were straining to contain and control so much wobbly flesh. He decided he'd call them Pinky and Perky. The pickles looked nice, but why pay that much when you don't even get a jar with a proper lid? There was Mrs Anderson; he had taught her daughter two or three years ago. Very nice girl; dreadful mother – voice absurdly loud. He moved along, keen to avoid a conversation.

Cheeses. *Maybe some Comte if they've got some*, he thought. Laura's favourite, ever since they had holidayed at Lacoste a few years ago. And as he scanned the table he caught sight of a face in profile and he instinctively smiled. But then he looked closer and felt his chest tighten a little and he stopped breathing. He turned away in shock, but then looked back over his shoulder, not daring to believe. She'd gone. He inhaled quickly and searched further to his right and she reappeared. It was her, surely? How long had it been? Forty years? The back of her head was the same shape; her hairstyle hadn't really changed – shoulder-length, naturally curling under. Lustrous still and no signs of grey either, unlike him. He looked at her clothes – bohemian skirt and cardigan still. Lovely ankles and blue espadrilles. He had to go up to her and say hello. What else would he say? She moved along towards the books. He could surely manage a conversation about books. He remembered *the* book, and what was written inside. Could see the handwriting even now. Her name. And a solitary kiss.

He moved around so he could approach her from the other side. He saw her again in profile, but then she turned her head so she was front on and he could see her eyes, the big, brown, inscrutable, beautiful, sparkling, tantalising eyes that had once looked at him, tormented him and taken his breath away. He then remembered her smell, and he inhaled, hoping to recapture the sensation. *Nearly*, he thought. He moved closer and saw the two small moles on her left arm. As she turned to move along to the next stall, she looked up and saw him looking at her. For a moment she looked away, perhaps mildly flattered that she was being stared at, but then she looked back, eyes wide, so wide, and smiled quizzically. *Brilliant double-take*, he thought.

'Hello, Jane.'

'How amazing! Goodness. Hello. How are you?'

'I'm fine, thanks. What are you doing *here?*'

'I'm here for a concert tonight. What about you?'

'I live here. Well, not here, but near here. But I do work here at the school. Teach here.'

'Really? I teach, too, in London. Singing, and the flute, of course.'

'Of course. I haven't forgotten. I've been here for thirty-five years. Sad, eh?'

She smiled, and looked at him, her brow slightly furrowed. He wondered if she was trying to remember what he had looked like forty years earlier, when they had last seen each other?

'I've missed you,' he said, and they both laughed. He thought it was quite a good line; unscripted, too. Her eyes became bigger and brighter and her smile revealed teeth that were no longer so white but which became instantly familiar again. Some wrinkles around the eyes and the lines down the side of her nose did nothing to spoil the elegant dignity of a face that he had once thought the most beautiful thing he had ever seen. Briefly he was elsewhere, in a past that he had never forgotten, in a pain he now could feel again, in a memory of some of the most intense moments of his life.

He needed to say something else. He wanted to reminisce, to see if she remembered everything, too. He wanted to be back there, back then. His stomach ached with the desire to be eighteen again. Like James. He looked at her again and suddenly he knew he had never stopped loving her. Suddenly so much of the literature he had been teaching for thirty-five years made more sense. He wanted to teach the texts one more time so that she could be his definitive and last Emma Woodhouse, Beatrice, Tess. She had always been his Lady Macbeth anyway. He thought he could feel a thin film of sweat start to come out at the top of his brow.

'Where are you going now?' She had come to his rescue and he silently chided himself for his adolescent intensity and his social awkwardness.

'I was about to go home, but what about you – what are you doing?'

'I have a choir rehearsal in the cathedral in a few minutes, but we'll be finished by 12.30.'

'Would you like to go for a coffee when you're finished? No, you'd prefer tea, wouldn't you? Maybe you have other plans?'

'No, I've no plans. And tea would be nice. Where shall we meet?'

They arranged to see each other at the north door of the cathedral, and she smiled again and walked off. He watched her move away, and remembered watching her walk away from him along the parched lawns alongside the Royal Shakespeare Theatre in Stratford. She was going to the stage door to get some autographs because it was nearly the 'half', and he was jealous of the actors. Had this been what she had intended? She was a little heavier now, but the stride was the same, the angle of her feet the same as she lifted them and then placed them confidently, purposefully; nobody was going to stop her. He saw the bottom of her calves and remembered staring at them in wonder once when they were picnicking on the cliffs on the north coast in Jersey – so smooth, such a lovely colour, just asking to be stroked and kissed. He saw her walking away from him at the airport. He remembered the two moles again, but then was surprised because he could not remember what her hands looked like. Her hands. Her hand. He found himself being taken back to the beginning.

3

FEBRUARY 1975

ON A BOAT TRAVELLING BETWEEN
JERSEY AND GUERNSEY

He knew it would happen because it had happened last time, too: he'd lost his bearings. He was looking left and right and up and down but simply couldn't remember on which deck he and the rest of the team had set up base. Why was his sense of direction so poor? Why was it clearly not remotely difficult for the others to find their way around? He felt queasy and the boat had only just left the harbour, hadn't even got beyond Elizabeth Castle. Would he be able to survive the crossing without being sick? Would he have to spend the rest of the journey on deck, hoping the sea breezes would help him keep down his porridge? How on earth could the team be expected to perform well against their bitter inter-insular rivals having endured a sea crossing like this one was promising to be? He sat in a vacant chair, his nausea not helped by the stickiness he could feel on the green leather seat and the dark wooden armrest, and tried to breathe slowly and deeply, hoping to sense even the slightest indication that he was feeling better.

A teammate was breezing past scoffing a bacon butty, the gently rocking ship no problem for him, some brown sauce dripping out of the bread onto his school blazer.

'Come on down, Phil. We're going to play three-card brag.' Philip had managed to get his dad to give him £5 for the day and he fancied his chances of winning some more, but he knew if he moved he'd be sick.

'Not feeling great, Graham. I'll stay here for a bit, thanks.' He was grateful his dad had given him the money. He thought he'd have to work really hard to persuade him, but for once his dad had handed over a crisp red Jersey £5 note without the lecture about Philip being an expensive luxury. On this occasion, he hadn't even bothered to mention his friend's son who had a master's degree but still couldn't get a job.

This dreadful boat. Why couldn't we fly? Philip thought queasily to himself, and then he smiled when he remembered outwitting his history teacher. Mr Chandler had said that you usually used the pronoun *she* when talking about ships. 'What about the mail boat?' Philip had asked, quick as a flash. Fair play to Chandler, though: he did laugh. And then he remembered Chandler had confined the comments he made on Philip's next essay to a single word – 'Unobjectionable'. At first he hadn't known what the word meant, though it wasn't exactly difficult if you broke it down, he realised later.

He started going through his lines in his head to try to distract himself from the ship's rolling movement. He'd been cast as Oberon in the school play, and hoped that silently reciting his words would preoccupy him and settle his stomach. He'd gone all the way through up to the last moments, staring throughout at a very dull painting of a nautical scene on the wall opposite. *Word-perfect*, he thought. He was remembering the song he had to sing at the end: '*To the best bride bed will we, / Which by us shall blessed be; / And the issue there create / Ever shall be fortunate.*' He'd rehearsed it with the head of music, and he sang it well in the bath. But he'd found when rehearsing it on stage that it never seemed to sit comfortably in his vocal range. And he had to be dancing at the same time – not his greatest talent. He knew it was all about confidence, really. He was anxious the scene would spoil his performance, and his nausea was threatening to return.

Three girls were coming down the stairs from the deck above, two with dark hair, another, slightly behind, very blonde. He looked at the first two. The shorter one looked slightly older than her companion. Friends? Sisters, perhaps. He was struck by their clothing, how many layers they were wearing, how it seemed designed to conceal their figures and femininity. And he noticed their lovely complexions, the olive skin, unblemished, and enormous, limpid brown eyes. They clearly did not notice the green-faced boy huddled in the corner, and down they went to the deck below.

He noticed that his breathing had changed; he was no longer breathing regularly to try to control his nausea. Instead he found himself holding his breath and feeling his heart beat in his chest. It reverberated in his head. *Is this how Romeo felt at the ball?* He was intrigued by the two girls and felt urgently that he needed to see her again, the older one, the leader. *Shall I follow them?* he wondered. *I can't. Apart from anything else I might be sick,* he told himself. *Will they come back up the stairs? Who are they? Why are they on the boat? What if I never see her again?*

He decided that if he willed it hard enough he could make her appear before he reached a hundred, counting slowly. He tried it, almost shocking himself by the intensity of his wish, aware of the absurdity of his behaviour but believing all the same that he could make her return. He kept counting, slowly, slowly. He waited and waited. The nausea had been replaced by a sickening sense of frustrated excitement, a certain knowledge that she would not reappear. He saw himself as the rejected suitor, the hero who doesn't win the girl but who smiles bravely and extends his very best wishes to her and her handsome and wealthy, but shallow, fiancé.

The boat finally docked, and a number of different queues were converging from various directions at the disembarkation platform. One last chance to see her again. A good chance, surely, with so many people gathered in one place. *This is how the film should end; or start.* But it wasn't to be. Instead, Graham appeared, eating a Mars bar and boasting that he'd won eight quid at brag.

They won the match 3-1. Philip had scored one of his team's goals, a header from a corner kick, but knew he hadn't had a very good game. But the boat journey back was always much better after a win, and the boys gathered in the bar, determined to blow whatever money they hadn't spent on the way over. Everyone was laughing at Andy who had said he wanted a Bacardi and Coke, *neat!* He'd already had three. Philip, too, was happily involved, no signs of nausea now, even though, or perhaps because, he was on his third vodka and lime.

He saw Corbiere lighthouse through one of the windows and decided he would go up on deck for the last few minutes while the boat sailed across St Brelade's Bay, Ouaisne and St Aubin's. He counted hundreds of the little bulbs strung along the promenade; watched the Dinky cars crawling along Victoria Avenue; saw his school perched on top of the hill, brilliantly and tastefully illuminated; and he tapped his hand on the deck rail in time with the flashing red lights guiding the boat into the harbour.

He surprised himself by finding his way to the embarkation deck without unwelcome detours and was standing in the queue waiting to get off and hoping his dad would be there to pick him up, like everyone else's dad would be. He would keep his cool if nobody was there, cheerfully decline any offers of a lift from other parents and head for the nearest phone box, halfway down the pier. He was concentrating intently on how he would not show embarrassment or disappointment. 'They're on the way,' he'd say. 'They should only be a couple of minutes.'

And then there she was. Three back in one of the other queues. The girl. Her companion just behind again, dutifully it seemed. Such a beautiful profile. High cheekbones; perfect straight nose; strong but delicate chin. Dignified. Elegant. Proud. He stared at her lips, and suddenly wanted desperately to kiss them. He wanted to touch her skin, to feel its smoothness. She looked in his direction and he caught her eye and tried to hold it. But she looked away, not out of embarrassment or a sense of modesty but simply because she hadn't actually seen him at all.

4

AUGUST 2018

SATURDAY
WORCESTER

Philip walked up the High Street, mildly concerned he would be later getting home than he had indicated. He sent a WhatsApp saying he had bumped into an old friend and wouldn't be back for lunch. *That's fine, I won't wait,* came the reply immediately. He thought about where to go for a cup of tea. Nowhere seemed right. He felt nervous, first-date apprehensive. Suddenly the sky seemed even bluer and the temperature higher, and he consciously tried to relax, desperate to avoid sweating into his mauve polo shirt. He tried to tell himself he was sixty years old and so was she and that his behaviour was puerile. But he was excited, animated in a way that opened every pore and made every step he took a movement of intense importance and physical joy. Every shop front was dazzling, each window displaying stylish, desirable products. The pyramids of soap bars had been sculpted immaculately; the shoes all looked so beautifully crafted and comfortable and he could tell the new leather would smell so gorgeous, like the new briefcase his dad had bought him when he started senior school; and the chocolates on display in gift boxes had been made by the world's most brilliant chocolatier, all of them a guaranteed sensation for the palate, even the coffee-flavoured ones he'd normally leave till last or hope someone else would choose. He had an hour to fill so headed for the bookshop.

He passed Nando's and looked through the windows to see if he could see James, but he couldn't. Eighteen years old. Everything to look forward to. Even without his parents' millions, James would be fine with his natural charm.

He moved on and suddenly felt a gentle but unstoppable wave of sadness roll over him, smothering the contentment he had felt just half an hour earlier. What had he actually achieved? As an eighteen-year-old, is this how he had imagined his life would unravel? He had influenced lots of young lives, he knew. He owned a car, a comfortable house – mortgage nearly paid off – and had a wonderful wife, who was his best friend and whom he loved and respected more than anyone else he knew, and two amazing sons whose successes and personalities he and Laura celebrated, all the while thinking how lucky they were. But what had he really accomplished? Every married man thought he had an amazing wife and brilliant children. Well, most anyway. As he stared at his reflection in the shop window, a short story he had often taught came into his mind, Ray Bradbury's *A Sound of Thunder*. Men travel back in time and one careless bloke treads on a butterfly. The impact millions of years later of that apparently insignificant event in the past is subtle but massive: a different US President has been elected; words are spelt differently; the invisible air feels strange somehow. And he asked himself how the world would be different if he had never existed, and how it would change when he died. And he knew that actually his life was basically not important. There'd be no obituary, no biography. His children would have photos, but they would quickly fade, or be stored away in the cloud, rarely, if ever, visited. He remembered the DVD he had in his classroom of *Death of a Salesman*, and the brilliant performance of Lee J Cobb as Willy Loman. He thought again about how he would love to play the part on stage, not just in the classroom. He started to see his own funeral, with nobody there except Laura, Tom and George. Not even a Charlie or a Bernard who go to Willy's.

But James was pleased to see me, Philip thought. He was happy to chat. *He'd remember me and so would dozens of others. Hundreds, maybe. Wouldn't they?* He breathed in deeply and looked up at a perfect blue sky. *Live for today*, he decided.

He walked into the bookshop, eschewed the elevator – *I'm not old*, he told himself – and climbed the stairs to the fiction department, insisting that he was feeling fit, strong and supple, his sometimes-troublesome knees feeling well-oiled and in perfect working order. *No, I'm not eighteen, but I'm not past it either.* He glanced at a poster advertising an outdoor production of *Romeo and Juliet*. He remembered her saying, 'You kiss by the book. Give me my kiss again.' He caught sight of a former colleague in the transport section, and immediately looked away and headed for the crime section. *Must be looking for something to do with trains*, he thought. He couldn't understand this enthusiasm. He didn't want to speak to him, didn't want to have to try to engage in a witty exchange, but didn't want to seem distracted or rude either, so he went back down, again taking the steps. Back on the ground floor, he saw a table of new releases and his eye was drawn to one particular title, *The Food of Love*. *Not much doubt where the inspiration for that title came from*, he thought, and as he picked it up to inspect it he was already feeling the throat-aching pain of rejection. He thought about the Bradbury story again: if he had trodden on a butterfly forty years earlier, how might his life have been different?

5

JANUARY 1976

JERSEY

Philip was working full-time in a gardening shop, wishing that he were still at school or, better still, already at university. He found the job incredibly dull, but the people he worked with were very kind and friendly. Most of the time he spent on the shop floor selling weed killers and packets of seeds. Occasionally he sold a garden fork or spade and there was a small thrill at having sold such an expensive item. It was a smelly shop and it wasn't much fun several times a day climbing the steep wooden stairs to the storeroom to fill a brown bag with bone meal or, worse still, dried blood. Lunchtimes were a welcome break, and he'd enjoy the forty-five minutes spent in the pub across the way, The Prince of Cumberland, eating a floppy white bread sandwich and drinking a pint of Mary Ann Best Bitter. His boss had happily given him permission to finish work early on Wednesdays and Fridays, at 3.30pm rather than 5.30pm, so he could walk through town up to his old school for rehearsals.

He walked into the school hall, a room so familiar to him because he had attended so many assemblies in there and had performed in school productions, including *A Midsummer Night's Dream* a year before. But today it felt so different: the old wooden chairs looked smaller and there seemed to be fewer of them; the stage at the west end seemed narrower and less elevated, and the portraits of Victoria and Albert, both looking imperiously down the hall, less imposing. And Philip wasn't wearing his school uniform. He was reflecting on how so much had changed since he had left school six months earlier, even though the hall had actually hardly changed in a hundred years.

A group of boys burst in noisily and dumped their bags on a row of chairs halfway back. Philip knew many of them. He was only a year older than most of them, after all, and had played in the same football and cricket teams as some. He felt a little awkward because he knew David – Mr Lyons, their English teacher – hadn't told them that he was going to be helping out. He found conversation difficult and so did they. Boys with whom he had shared schoolboy jokes and under-age drinks suddenly seemed like strangers, rather young and immature. Some common ground was found when a couple of them started to talk about the football tour they'd been on before the end of the previous term. Philip had experienced two of these himself and was not remotely surprised by their stories of excess. It suddenly went quiet. David – the boys called him Mr Lyons to his face, but Lionel when he wasn't there or couldn't hear – walked in, looking dapper with his yellow handkerchief flopping casually from his jacket pocket. He was wearing socks which all of his pupils had seen before and found amusing, the bright yellow matching the pocket handkerchief but not really going with the formal grey pin-striped suit. *Malvolio yellow*, Philip thought, and he wondered if David had chosen them deliberately.

David asked everyone to sit down and he told the boys how Philip was going to be involved. He made Philip sound important and the boys didn't seem to smirk, share glances or hide smiles behind their hands, and Philip felt not only relieved but quietly confident that he was going to be able to justify his participation in the project and to enjoy himself.

Suddenly there was a big cheer as three girls walked in. They had come from the sister school across town, and this was the earliest they would be able to get to rehearsals, ten minutes after the boys. The boys knew who they were – they would have met the girls at the auditions and had probably been socialising with them all year anyway.

'Ah, the real talent has arrived,' David proclaimed in all innocence. The boys guffawed, of course. Philip didn't even smile, not because of any great maturity or sense of responsibility but because the girl he had last seen on the boat had just suddenly reappeared in his world. He knew it was her instantly and his stomach lurched, almost as if he were back on board. David formally introduced the girls to the rest of the cast and to Philip, and Philip learnt that the girl on the boat was called Jane. He was aware that he had looked at her for longer than necessary when introduced so resolved hardly to look at her at all during the rehearsal that was shortly to start. But this was going to prove difficult because David said he himself would work on the first scene with Orsino, Valentine, Curio and attendant lords, and Philip should look at the first Olivia and Viola meeting in the space already cleared at the other end of the hall. The boys did their best, but failed, Philip thought, to conceal their disappointment that their rehearsal wasn't going to involve Jane.

He was thrown by this sudden turn of events but couldn't believe his luck. He was going to rehearse with her, with Jane Thomas, and it was his favourite scene in the play. He remembered counting to a hundred and she hadn't reappeared. But she had now. Slowly he regained some composure, and he started to feel confident he would be able to conduct a useful rehearsal.

'OK, then. Let's see what we can do with this scene. Jane, tell me what you think of Olivia.' Philip had surprised himself by asking her such a direct question.

'She's in deep mourning and wants to be allowed to grieve in peace, without being disturbed by troublesome suitors.'

'And yet by the end of this scene she seems to have forgotten she's in mourning, doesn't she? The veil has been lifted. What might this suggest about her mourning?' He paused, but she stayed silent. 'How old do you think she is?'

Jane seemed a little put out by Philip's challenging of what she had said and also surprised by the question about her age. She maintained her poise as best she could, but he thought he saw a glint of something fiery in her eyes and a tiny red flush on her neck. It was a beautiful neck, set off by her brilliant white blouse, the collar of which sat so naturally elegantly and stylishly. He thought with shame of his own very limited wardrobe and how envious he felt of people who seemed so comfortable in their clothes and who didn't need to make any effort to look good. Or stunning.

He noticed that Jane was now looking directly at him, almost defiantly.

'She's very young, I think.'

He was anxious to agree, keen not to alienate her or to sound arrogant. 'Yes, it's adolescent behaviour, isn't it, and what we see in this scene is how quickly her behaviour changes because she is falling for Cesario. The *veil* is lifted, as I said, and also the *mask* is taken off.' Jane said nothing. Perhaps she nodded, but it was scarcely perceptible. He became aware that so far there had been no discussion with Harriet about Viola.

'OK. So, Harriet, what about Viola? What is her motivation in this scene? What does she think of Olivia?'

Harriet proceeded to articulate a full Coles Notes character study of Viola and Philip found himself not listening, and instead thinking first about the red flush on Jane's neck and then how he would be able to impress her with his direction and then how he needed to accept the fact that the scene was as much about Viola, of course, as Olivia. He was aware that Harriet had stopped talking, and said, 'Fine, great, let's see what happens if we try to work the scene. And Harriet, your name is V*io*la, not Vi*o*la. Don't stress the wrong syllable.' As soon as he'd made the feeble joke he wished he hadn't, especially when he thought he heard Jane sigh with a combination of condescension and boredom.

Philip let the scene begin, biting his tongue to stop himself pointing out to Harriet that '*exquisite*' should be stressed on the first syllable and not the second. Both of the girls were good and Philip could see why David had cast them. Harriet made Viola entirely committed on Orsino's behalf, thus ensuring she was admirable and sympathetic. She also seemed to have that remarkable gift of sounding convincing even if she didn't always understand what she was saying. Jane seemed to have processed and absorbed what Philip had said earlier about Olivia's youth. The moment when Olivia agreed to Viola's request to let her see her face made Philip's heart leap. He suggested to Harriet that she simply stare at Jane's face in awe and he allowed himself a wonderful few seconds of doing so himself. When Harriet spoke the lines, '*Lady, you are the cruell'st she alive / If you will lead these graces to the grave / And leave the world no copy*,' Philip found himself imagining being in bed with Jane. He was lost, until he heard Jane say, '*But yet I cannot love him*,' at which point he dismissed the vision and immediately caught her eye. They were coming towards the end of the scene, and Philip felt absurdly jealous when Jane portrayed Olivia's delighted confusion when recognising she was falling in love with Cesario. He was about to stop her to talk about her reference to *the plague* when David called from the other end of the hall to suggest the two groups come together to see each other's work. Philip couldn't help noticing how Jane immediately started talking easily to her fellow students, all of whom seemed to gravitate towards her, keen to secure her attention. He knew she had not the remotest interest in him. And now she was in particularly earnest conversation with Tony, who was playing Sebastian. Tony looked spellbound.

JANUARY 1976
JERSEY

It was two Fridays later and Philip was rehearsing again. He had been working on the scene in which Sir Toby and Fabian try to get Sir Andrew and Viola to fight, not his favourite scene and not the easiest. Throughout the rehearsal he had been looking forward to the short exchange at the end between Olivia and Sebastian, desperate to be working again with Jane. But he had worked hard to prepare the fight scene and hoped he had impressed the watching Jane with his ideas and his management of the blocking and the choreography.

Finally they got to Olivia's entrance, and they worked the short exchange, at the end of which Philip suggested that Olivia should kiss Sebastian when he agrees to be 'rul'd' by her. He was expecting to see a nervous, schoolboy/schoolgirl peck on the lips and was shocked when Jane and Tony not only immediately agreed with the idea but also then proceeded to kiss each other without any awkwardness at all and at some length. *It is as if they have done this before*, Philip thought, with a sickening feeling in his stomach. *I bet they have.* He felt he had been betrayed, before reluctantly accepting he had no right to, and had no grounds whatsoever for feeling cheated. He had only ever spoken to her in rehearsal, as director to actress. He knew nothing about her. She clearly had no recollection of their brief encounter on the boat and why should she? He knew he was being ridiculous – immature, self-indulgent and irrational. The kiss over, she looked at Philip, her expression quietly but unmistakably saying to him: 'That showed you, didn't it!' He looked again at her lips. He knew that *he* had caught *'the plague'*; he had fallen in love.

Somehow he managed to get through what was left of the rehearsal, trying to put on a brave face, but it was so hard to smile when his heart was feeling something else. After all, he was the one who had already left school; he was the one who should be able to rise above schoolboy crushes. But his hopes sank even further at the end of the rehearsal when he saw Tony and Jane holding hands as they left the hall, Jane pulling him along as if he were her spaniel.

FEBRUARY 1976
JERSEY

Philip had been looking forward so much to the end of his working week. He had spent the mornings in the shop but every day after lunch had been driven to a large field in St Martin, a more northern parish, where he and an older worker between them were planting an orchard for the owner of the shop. The ten-minute journey in the dusty old white van with the clanking exhaust was the best part of the afternoon because it was warm and easy. Working in the field was cold and exhausting. They had nine hundred fruit trees to plant in a grid formation. His fellow worker, Alf, a proud Jerseyman, well-known locally for his own award-winning garden at home, told Philip why the holes were about two feet deep and placed six yards apart, with six yards left between rows, but Philip, though trying to listen politely, wasn't interested. Alf told him why the soil in the field was ideal for the apple trees they were planting, but again Philip didn't really hear the explanation.

They worked one row at a time. A stake had to be driven vertically into the bottom of the hole, using a sledgehammer. Alf was driving the tractor into position, then he would leave the wheel to climb into the trailer where there were stakes and young fruit trees. With the stake in position, the tree would be placed adjacent to it, about six inches distant, downwind of the stake so that the prevailing wind (usually a south-westerly) would blow the tree away from the stake. The stakes extended about four feet above ground level and the trees were tied to them so that the stems of the trees were about six inches from the stake. Alf was doing all the hard work while Philip first held the stake upright and then the tree. Some fertiliser was then tipped into the hole and Philip had to mix it with the topsoil that he then shovelled in to bed the trees' roots. It was mind-numbing work and the freezing weather made it a real test of endurance. The prospect of the mid-afternoon break when they went into the barn for a cup of tea and biscuits was the only thing that kept Philip going. He wanted the kettle to take longer to boil to bring the slowly approaching darkness closer. But they always went back out. He tried to hold the stakes so that there was a gap between his gloves and the sleeve of his sweater, meaning he could see his watch, and at times he felt that not only did the minute hand not move but neither did the second hand. He remembered descriptions of Levin in *Anna Karenina*, which David had recommended he read, working on the land and being so absorbed that his exhaustion was almost a spiritual experience. Philip tried to imagine he was Levin, but he failed because he found the work almost unbearable, causing pain and discomfort and never any spiritual nourishment. When 4.30 arrived and it was becoming too dark and dangerous to work, he would perversely savour the planting of the last tree of the day because it meant he could anticipate the sheer joy of stopping. Someone had told him once that anticipation was seventy-five per cent of the pleasure. He didn't quite agree, but working in that orchard was certainly helping him at least to understand the concept.

At the end of the working week he was anticipating a night out with two friends. They were still at school, in the upper sixth, but one had been a teammate in the school's football and cricket First XIs, and both were in *Twelfth Night*, Andy playing Antonio and Terry playing the priest, neither of them glamorous roles, but both mates were pleased simply to be involved because school plays were great fun and actually pretty cool.

For a change they had decided to go to the St Mary's Inn, just a few hundred yards from where Philip lived. Both Andy and Terry had cars, and on this occasion Andy had agreed to pick up Terry. Philip made his way down the road, past the pig farm, and past the chapel, feeling much better after his hot bath, though his hands still ached from all the holding and lifting and fork and spade work. Arriving first, he ordered a pint of Mary Ann and sat down in a cosy corner close to the open fire. He was staring at the swirling red patterned carpet, much of it stiff from years of spilt beer, but thinking of Jane, and in particular whether or not he should send her a Valentine's Day card. And if he did send one, what should he write? He was enjoying the sweet torment of his own indecision. How could he make it anonymous but make sure she knew it was from him? Could he come up with something witty? Or was it simply better not to send one and to be able to dream on, unrejected? Andy and Terry knew about his obsession: he'd ask them what they'd do.

They were all on their third pint, and Terry said, 'Don't muck about. Just ask her out, tell her she'd be mad to say no and get on with it.' He then took three huge gulps of beer, half emptying what had been a full glass. Andy, more cerebral and more circumspect, lacking confidence and experience like Philip himself, started to think about what Philip could write, reeling off a number of literary quotations. 'What about, "*You're a damned attractive woman, Jane,*"' he suggested, channelling his best Major Magnus from Tom Stoppard's *The Real Inspector Hound*. Terry laughed, and Philip himself was not unamused. 'Or you could be Darcy.'

'Who?' Terry asked.

'Go on – what do you mean?' Philip asked.

'"*In vain I have struggled. It will not do. My feelings will not be repressed. You must allow me to tell you how ardently I admire and love you,*"' Andy said.

'And how ardently I would like to shag you,' Terry added.

'I think I prefer the Jane Austen,' Philip said.

'I don't,' Terry retorted. 'My version is more honest and to the point. Or you could use the Jane Austen and then add my bit at the end. Best of both worlds. Bit of bollocks and then what you really mean.'

'Yes, thanks a lot, Terry. That's that sorted then. Do you think you could manage to write a sonnet for me too?' Philip asked.

'I could manage a limerick or two,' Terry offered. All three of them laughed, and Philip got up, collected the three glasses and went to the bar. He ordered more beer. Part of him wished he had Terry's uncomplicated confidence, but he knew he could never be like that. And anyway, it wasn't really about the shagging, was it? Should he or shouldn't he send a Valentine's card? *If it should fail?* he asked himself. He decided to proceed no further with the idea.

MARCH 1976
JERSEY

It was the night of the last performance. The cast were getting dressed excitedly and having their make-up done. Philip was wandering around checking everyone was all right and giving one or two last-minute notes, particularly to Harriet who had rushed the *'willow cabin'* speech last night. He found himself doing the speech for her before remembering what a famous director had once said – he couldn't remember who: 'A bad director tells you what to do; and the worst director shows you how to do it.' So he stopped himself 'performing' and simply encouraged her not to waste the words, not to forget that while delivering the words to Olivia she could imagine she's delivering them to Orsino.

'Thanks, Philip. That's actually a really helpful idea. I'm going to try that tonight.'

He was really chuffed to receive such grateful thanks and felt a surge of pride and satisfaction as he realised that the cast had truly accepted him, basically one of their peers, as their director. He breathed deeply and turned to head towards the corner where Jane was. He saw her in earnest conversation with Tony. Neither looked happy. Jane was sitting down in front of a mirror brushing her hair quite roughly while Tony seemed to be seeking from her some kind of explanation that she was not prepared to give. Philip thought it best to leave them to it, but he was keen to find out what had caused the tension between them. He looked around and saw Paul, Malvolio, who made a rather theatrical gesture suggesting nobody ought to get too close to Tony and Jane. Philip edged towards Paul, and whispered, 'What's going on there?'

'Lovers' tiff.'

'It had better not spoil their performances,' Philip said, rather pleased with himself for making the production sound like his only concern. He glanced back at Paul and suddenly realised that his indifference to the lovers' tiff was also merely a façade; he would surely try to move in when the opportunity arose.

He had hoped the last night would be a really memorable occasion, but Philip was wincing in the wings at every little verbal slip, and he was convinced the audience weren't laughing as much and weren't as engaged as they had been on the previous two nights. David seemed to think it was going very well, the best performance of the three. Philip was particularly keen to see the Olivia/Sebastian scenes. It came to the kiss and there was no doubt that it was much shorter than it had been and it was clear that Jane had been the one to break it off. He was sure he could see her set her jaw behind an unconvincing smile. Philip decided that his feelings for Jane were stronger than his hopes that the performance would be a triumph. He knew, not unaware of his selfishness, that he'd be happy to accept forgotten lines, costume malfunctions, late entrances if after the show Jane would smile at him, hold his hand, offer her lips to be kissed.

The cast party on stage followed, with the usual presentations and speeches and bottles of Coke, lemonade and Asti. Philip noticed how Tony and Jane stood on different sides of the stage, Tony visibly miserable and Jane, pinched mouth, looking determined to maintain her poise. He was delighted to receive a signed card and a pair of cricket bat cufflinks as a present from the cast. All he needed now was a shirt with which he could wear them. David was given a bottle of St Emilion. Philip preferred the cufflinks. He knew that the cast would go off to a pub in town after the party while he and David had a final glass of Asti and did the clearing-up. He was desperate to know if Jane would be going with the rest of them. Various boys and girls made a point of thanking him for what he had done to help them and for the opportunities they'd been given and the enormous fun they'd had. Jane approached him. Would she smile? What could he say? This might be the last time he saw her.

'Thank you, Philip,' she said. 'I enjoyed rehearsals and learnt a lot from you.'

'I don't imagine you enjoyed the rehearsals as much as I did. It was a pleasure to work with you.' Why couldn't he say what he really wanted to say? Was it really so difficult to ask her if she'd like to go for a drink sometime? Yes, it was. He just couldn't say it. She smiled and walked away, and as he saw her recede into the distance, he said, 'I love you.' But not out loud.

He arrived home shortly after midnight. He felt exhausted and his back ached, having spent the last few hours standing in the wings watching and then stuck like a barman behind the drinks table at the after-show party. He washed his hands and face and cleaned his teeth, staring intently and pulling faces in the mirror in the way only someone who has had too much to drink does. He sat in bed and opened the envelope containing the thank-you card from the cast. The picture on the front was of a director's chair, with a director on a film set shouting through a megaphone at his cast. The back of the chair had a blank space in it in which someone had written, 'Phil'. He liked the balance of cheekiness and friendliness. There was also a speech bubble coming out of the megaphone in which someone had written, 'CHANGE THE PICTURE!', one of his favourite instructions when directing. He looked inside, deliberately trying to avoid finding Jane's name because he wanted to save that until last. A number had simply signed their names – some very neatly, some with a Hollywood flamboyance – while some of the principals had written genuinely thoughtful words. He smiled when he saw Harriet's contribution: 'Thanks, Phil. You were EXcellent, EXtremely inspirational, in fact absolutely "EXquisite" Ex, Ex, Ex'.

He now turned to the bottom right of the inside page of the card where he had unavoidably noticed Jane had signed, 'Thank you. All good wishes, Jane.' *'All good wishes'? What? What was that supposed to mean? Was she a spinster parishioner with wrinkly tights writing to the vicar?* He'd got 'lots of love' from Feste, and four kisses from Fabian, for Christ's sake! He stared at her words, trying to make them say something else, trying to find something cryptic. But he couldn't. The five blandest words ever written. *'I suppose him virtuous, know him noble, / …In voices well divulged, free, learn'd and valiant, / And in dimension and the shape of nature / A gracious person; BUT YET I CANNOT LOVE HIM.'* He had one more look to see if her words on the card had changed or if there were some more somewhere he hadn't noticed. No. He knew he was being dramatic and ridiculous, and he knew he had drunk too much Asti, but he still threw the card onto the floor, mumbling the words, *'Farewell, fair cruelty.'*

6

AUGUST 1976

JERSEY

His friend Andy had received his A level results and would be taking up his place at Oxford. There hadn't been any doubt because he'd only had to get two Es, but the three As were cause for celebration and they certainly intended to celebrate in style, if an evening drinking pints at The Royal in St Martin could be considered stylish.

Philip was admiring his shirt in the mirror. His mum had given it to him. She worked for an incredibly wealthy young woman, only ten years older than him, whose husband threw clothes out after he'd had them a few months, even though they were still in beautiful condition. Philip and his mum joked that he changed his car as often as he changed his clothes, simply because the ashtray was full. His mum had passed on the shirt and a pair of very smart brogues the last time he'd been to see her. She lived in a beautiful little cottage on the estate of her employer, a couple of miles away from where he lived with his dad. The shirt fitted perfectly. He was admiring the pattern of cerise and damselfly blue swirls, the precise stitching and the crispness of the enormous collar and was trying to decide whether to leave two buttons or three undone at the top. He was particularly pleased with the Harrods label.

He heard the telephone ring downstairs, knew he was alone in the house, and rushed to get to it before it rang off.

'81823.'

'Hello, Philip. David Lyons here. Do you have a minute?'

'Hello, David. Yes, of course.' He knew Andy would be arriving shortly to pick him up and a conversation with David, which never lasted only a minute, wasn't really what he wanted.

'I have a plan in which you feature.'

'This sounds interesting. Tell me more.' *But make it quick,* Philip thought.

'I am putting on a play on September 25, 26 and 27 in the school theatre and I would like you to be in it.'

There was a pause, Philip waiting for David to elaborate. And hoping he'd get on with it, as he glanced at his watch. But David was silent, probably expecting to encounter some enthusiasm.

'That would be just before I go off to Birmingham, wouldn't it? OK, so what's the play?'

'It's *A Streetcar Named Desire*, and I want you to play the male lead, Stanley Kowalski.'

'Obviously I've heard of it, but I don't know anything about it.'

'It's a gritty 1940s American play; very modern, very powerful and also very beautiful and profoundly moving. Stanley Kowalski is a brutal working-class figure who rapes his sister-in-law while she is staying in the apartment where he lives with his pregnant wife. So obviously you've been typecast.'

'Oh yes, just like Oberon, isn't he?'

'Could be his twin.'

Philip looked again at his watch. 'That sounds really exciting, David. Thank you. Look, sorry about this, but I've got to go. Andy is about to come to pick me up. We're going to the pub to celebrate his results.'

'Yes, he did well, didn't he? As expected, of course. All right, I'll let you go. But you may like to know that Jane Thomas, the girl who played Olivia, has accepted the invitation to play Blanche, the female lead, and her sister is going to play her sister in the play, which will be quite amusing and very effective, I hope. And, actually, the other reason I rang is to ask if you'd like to come to supper on Saturday to read some of the play together and to talk about it. Jane has already said she'd like to come. I offered to pick up both of you, but Jane has said she would very happily drive you both. You might like to give her a ring to make arrangements.'

Suddenly the evening out with Andy seemed fantastically uninteresting. Philip told David he'd love to join him on Saturday, said he'd contact Jane, and then apologised for rushing off.

'All good wishes.' He still had the card in a drawer. Her words hadn't changed. And neither had his feelings.

He checked he had his money in his pocket and left the house, walked round to the road and sat on the wall to wait for Andy. He stared down the road, looking for the approach of Andy's blue Morris 1100 but seeing only the beautiful face of Jane Thomas as she thanked him when she left the *Twelfth Night* party.

He guessed that not many people had ever chosen the phone book as bedtime reading. But Philip was sitting up in bed, telephone directory, pen and pad in front of him. It really didn't need to be done before tomorrow, but when he got back from The Royal, too many pints later and Andy's and others' successes having been celebrated increasingly raucously by an ever-growing group of friends, all of them in good spirits, even those with disappointing results, Philip was able to focus on what he had wanted to be thinking about all evening.

He knew where Jane lived and he was able to find her number in the phone book even though there were enough Thomases for a Cardiff directory. He wrote down the number and then tried to think of what he would say when he called her home tomorrow. There was so much to consider. Who would pick up the phone? Would her sister or her parents know who he was? Would he recognise her voice if she answered? Had she really offered to pick him up, or had David got the wrong end of the stick? It had been known. How embarrassing would that be? Would she perhaps ring him? Just imagine. He knew he wouldn't be able to sleep as he contemplated spending the following morning both waiting for a call and building up the courage to make one. But he was wrong: the beer quickly worked its evil magic.

When he woke up, he immediately thought of Jane. He looked out of his bedroom window at the field with the horse in and further to his right at the larger field in which when he was younger there had occasionally been gymkhanas. He had often used this field to practise hitting golf balls; it was wide enough to accommodate extreme slices and spectacular hooks. Just as well. He remembered the previous Christmas holiday when he'd had a job for a fortnight delivering flowers on a special bicycle with huge panniers and a small trailer, and one morning he'd taken a bouquet to Tony Jacklin's house. It had amused him so much when Jacklin himself had answered the door because he was wearing a beautiful cream Pringle V-neck pullover but had spilt tomato ketchup down it.

His thoughts quickly returned to telephoning Jane. He decided it would be unseemly to call before 10.30am, the precise time plucked out of a book of etiquette he had created in his mind. He imagined her parents: correct, ferociously intelligent, disarmingly well-read, fastidious and effortlessly charming. Strikingly good-looking: the Byronic father; the mother like Charlotte Rampling.

He rehearsed his opening speech and cringed as he heard how unnatural and over-prepared it sounded. Embarrassed by his own pathetic intensity, he headed for the bathroom and tried to shake himself out of it by splashing cold water over his face. Back in his room, he dressed in front of the mirror, fully aware that his efforts to dress carefully and to make his hair look natural by running his fingers through it several times were not strictly necessary given that the telephone was a means of communicating orally, not visually.

He couldn't manage to finish his bowl of cornflakes, even though after a beery night he would normally eat enough to satisfy a greedy family of six. He tried to read the newspaper. He'd recently persuaded his dad to subscribe to *The Times* because David had recommended he read a broadsheet instead of the *Daily Mirror*. But he was taking nothing in so decided he'd walk up the road for half an hour and then back, by which time it would nearly be time to ring.

He had walked as far as St Mary's Church, where his dad's parents were buried. He recalled the evening with Andy and Terry in the pub across the road when he had agonised over whether or not to send Jane a Valentine's card, and he tried to recite the obscene limerick Terry had composed that evening: 'There once was a girl from Arabia'.

He walked the long way back, up towards his primary school and then turning right to walk along what his mum had always called 'The Dangerous Road' to dissuade him from taking that route home from school. It didn't seem dangerous to him now, over ten years later. He turned right again past the entrance to the pig farm and then left and was soon back home. It was still only 10.05.

He collected his pad and pencil and placed them on the windowsill by the phone. Having decided that waiting until precisely 10.30 to call would seem too studied, too deliberate, he started to prepare himself to call earlier. He surprised himself by lifting up the receiver and dialling, only starting to panic when he heard the ringing tone.

'Hello, Margaret Thomas speaking.'

'Oh, hello, Mrs Thomas. It's Philip Robinson here. Is it possible to speak to Jane, please?'

'Hello, Philip. Yes, of course. I'll get her for you straight away.' *Not stuffy at all*, Philip thought. *And she seems to know who I am.* He heard a bellowing call, and imagined Mrs Thomas was calling for Jane up the stairs. The hand in his jeans pocket was clenched into a very tight fist. He could hear someone coming quickly down a flight of stairs.

'Hello?'

'Hello, Jane. It's Philip Robinson.'

'Oh, hello. I was going to ring you later.'

'Ah. Well. Um, I gather from David Lyons that you have offered to give me a lift to his house tomorrow evening to talk about *A Streetcar Named Desire*.'

'Yes. Would that help? David said he didn't think you were driving yet. I've only just passed my test and I need to practise as much as possible and I thought this would be a good chance.'

'Well, that would be great. Thanks very much. I've had two lessons with my dad in the car park at Le Braye but will need a few proper ones before I take my test, I think. So, yes please. What time will you pick me up? Actually, do you know where I live?'

'I think we're expected at David's at 7.30 and he lives at

Gorey, doesn't he? I know you live somewhere in St Mary's, don't you, so shall we say seven o'clock? Now where exactly are you?'

Philip was able to give clear directions because there were obvious landmarks, and Jane was very confident she'd be able to find him.

'See you tomorrow at seven then.'

'Yes, thank you very much, Jane. Bye.'

'Bye, then.'

And that was it.

He didn't think he'd made a fool of himself. But it wasn't exactly a long conversation, was it? Less than a minute. *'But yet I cannot love him.'* 'All good wishes'. He noticed sweat marks had started to spread in both armpits. He wouldn't want that in her car tomorrow or at David's house. What could he wear to minimise the risk? He realised he'd intended to discuss dress code with Jane, but he'd forgotten. It was all right for her: she looked wonderful in everything. He thought he could wear the Harrods shirt again if he washed it, and he immediately went back to his room to retrieve it from the back of the chair at his desk. If he washed it by hand it probably wouldn't need ironing.

With Karen Carpenter singing 'Sometimes' on his little cassette recorder, and the shirt and his hands soaking in the bathroom wash hand basin, he experienced a moment of detachment and asked himself: *Why does someone you hardly know mean so much to you?* He thought that above all else it was because he found her face so beautiful. He had read somewhere about the golden ratio proportions in the human face, but he had no idea if Jane's features conformed. If they didn't, the ratio was clearly wrong. He remembered how he had been stunned when he first saw her face for those fleeting moments on the boat. And it was a gorgeous agony remembering those moments when he stared at her during one of the first *Twelfth Night* rehearsals. He looked at himself in the mirror above the basin. Freckles, almost no spots, thank goodness, a wonky smile. But Jane's complexion was perfect in colour and texture, and he just knew it was entirely natural and that she had no need of dermatological secrets. And her eyes – chestnut sheen inviting all his hopes and dreams and desires, and suggesting so much behind their tantalising inscrutability. And the lips he would give anything to kiss: perfect Cupid's bow, not too full, not too thin, elegant in both shape and proportion. Evolution should stop now.

Philip knew, too, that her unattainability was part of what made her so compelling; he was Orsino to her Olivia, but an Orsino for whom no shipwrecked Viola would ever appear. He dreamt of living with her forever, as lovers, as husband and wife, as parents, as best friends, never to be parted, reading poetry with her and listening to her play and sing.

She meant so much to him because she was everything he could ever want and because, quite simply, he loved her and always would.

He noticed his hands had grown red and swollen in the hot soapy water and the colours of his shirt looked even more vivid and intense. He pulled the plug and ran the cold tap to rinse away the suds, enjoying the sensation of the water on his hands and not minding when he managed to splash half a basin down the front of his jeans.

It was only 6.40pm but already Philip was sitting on the wall outside his house waiting for Jane. He was admiring the profusion of deep red roses on the gable wall and wondering why he had never really noticed them before even though he had walked past them hundreds of time over the years. What an astonishing colour. An incredible display of poetry in a setting that was otherwise so prosaic. They were never tended, fed or pruned – they were just nature doing what nature does. *'For women are as roses whose fair flower, / Being once displayed, doth fall that very hour.'* But not Jane: she would be beautiful forever. He caught the scent of his aftershave. He'd been given a selection box of Aramis products as a birthday present and still had plenty of the eau de cologne left. He hadn't put on too much and hoped she'd like it, hoped it was subtle and discreet.

What on earth is a streetcar? Why would a streetcar be called 'Desire'? Would he be raping Jane or her sister? Surely it would have to happen off-stage. It was going to have to be a pretty intensive rehearsal period to get the thing ready in not much more than a month. He'd be seeing Jane very regularly, or maybe they wouldn't have that many scenes together. *But surely the male and female leads must have. Although Romeo and Juliet don't have that many.*

He'd been imagining she would arrive in a smart shiny vehicle so was surprised when she pulled up in an old red Mini, the paintwork on the roof sun-bleached to a dusty pink. *Deep breath.* He jumped off the wall, opened the door and got in.

'Hello. Thanks very much for this, Jane. This is so much out of your way.' She'd smiled at him as he got in and now he looked at her profile. His heart started aching immediately.

'I've enjoyed the drive. Any chance to practise is much appreciated, so thank you for living where you do. I haven't been in this part of the island very often. These lanes look lovely, especially in gorgeous sunshine like this.' He noticed a little red flush on her neck, and he swallowed and caught his breath. *Maybe she isn't as relaxed as she appears to be,* he thought. She was wearing a little lip-gloss. Evolutionary perfection with some cosmetic enhancement. *Don't stare,* he told himself.

'Do you know the best way to David's from here?' he asked.
'Think so.'

'Good. I can help if need be, though I'm not usually very good at directions.'

He wanted to look at her legs. She was wearing a pink and white floral dress; Philip thought it might be called a pinafore dress. And it was hitched up so that her knees were showing. He pretended to look all around the inside of the car so that he could justify glancing at her legs, and he allowed his eyes to rest on them for a few seconds. He realised he was less than two feet away from them and he could so easily reach across and touch her knees. He thought she must have been aware of his stare because she asked, 'So, what do you think of *Streetcar*?'

'Sorry, of what?'

'*Streetcar*. The play, *A Streetcar Named Desire*.'

'To be honest, I don't really know it. Let me re-phrase that: I don't know it at all.'

'Oh, I did it for A level.'

'Oops. Sorry, just realised. I should have asked. Um, was Thursday a good day for you?'

'A very good day, thank you. As in English and music, and a B in French, and my deferred place at Durham is already confirmed.'

'Better than me last year. But of course history is much harder than music.'

'It certainly is not!' She looked fierce, but then smiled.

'Anyway, well done. And phew. I don't suppose you would have much fancied re-visiting the play if the English result had been different?'

'Probably not, but I'm really excited about playing Blanche. I love the play. You'll love it too. Everyone loves *Streetcar*.'

Philip had just started to notice her smell. Fresh, discreet, pastel green. He realised too that he had just had his longest-ever conversation with her and it had happened quite naturally.

'You smell nice,' she said. 'What is it?'

'Aramis. You smell nice, too.'

'I'm not wearing any perfume.'

'You still smell nice.' It had just come out, but when she smiled, he was pleased he'd said it. 'Go on then, tell me what it's about so that I won't look a complete idiot when we get to David's.'

'That's not easy. Well, it's a play of antinomies.'

'I'm delighted to hear that. Are they anything like arch-enemies?'

'Very good. No. Well, in a way, yes, actually. The play is about conflicts.'

'All plays are about conflicts.'

'Yes, I know, but this one is about battles for supremacy between old and new, poetry and prose, hot baths and cold showers, male and female, polka music and the hot trumpet, idealism and pragmatism, death and desire.'

'Is that all? Not much to it, then! OK, so what is a streetcar and why is it called "Desire"?'

'You must know what a streetcar is!'

'Absolutely, but I like listening to you.' She looked across at him, tilting her head a little, as though she were looking over non-existent spectacles. He'd surprised himself again, felt a tingle around his tongue and gulped. He noticed that she was smiling, in her eyes too, and he smiled inside and felt his heart ticking excitedly.

'It's a tram. The play is set in New Orleans, and there used to be a tram there that really was called Desire. Probably still is. But the title is quite a sophisticated metaphor actually. You'll see.'

'OK, so you say one of the aunty thingies is between male and female. Who wins?'

'Haha. Good question. Given that the heroine gets carted off to a loony bin at the end because the bloke has raped her on the night his wife is giving birth to their son, you could argue that the woman loses. But the bloke is an ape and a complete bastard. Trouble is, his wife adores him.'

'Does she know he's raped this other woman?'

'Her sister. Yes, I believe she does.'

'Why does she adore him, then?'

'"*There are things that happen between a man and a woman in the dark*"...' She looked across at him and raised her eyebrows.

He swallowed again and quietly took a slow, deep breath. She changed gear to slow down at a T-junction, and he saw her hitch her dress a little higher.

'Well, I can't imagine what those things are. And, um, which part are you playing, the wife or the sister-in-law?'

'The sister-in-law. So, you rape me and have very exciting sex with my sister.'

'Is there a Disney version of this?'

'I suspect not!'

'To be honest, I can't see the attraction of the part.' She looked at him and they both smiled. They were both enjoying the banter. She seemed different already from the 'All good wishes' incarnation.

There was a short period of companionable silence until Philip said, 'It's just on the right after that row of parked cars. Do you see those white gates? He's opened them for us.'

'Have you been here before?'

'Yes, I came just before we started *Twelfth Night*, and on a couple of occasions after Friday rehearsals. You can park just there, alongside David's Toyota.'

David was at the door to greet them both and led them through the hall and then the sitting room onto a small terraced area that afforded beautiful views of Grouville Bay and Mont Orgueil Castle.

'Welcome, welcome, welcome. Sit yourselves down. Philip, you pour the wine while I pop briefly to the kitchen. I'll be with you in a minute.'

He lifted the bottle from a damp earthenware container and dutifully poured the wine, trying to work out what the container was for.

Jane stared out at the bay and recited, "*The sea is calm tonight. / The tide is full*"—'

'I can't see the moon yet, but that is indeed the French coast.' Jane looked at him, clearly impressed. 'We did *Dover Beach* for A level, too,' he explained. 'But I *do* believe in a land of dreams, in joy, in love, in light.' And he turned to her and held her gaze and recited, "*Ah love, let us be true / To one another.*"' David's approach became audible, and Philip quickly said, 'Sorry, Jane. Miles away for a moment then.'

'Was it somewhere nice?'

'Oh yes.'

'You're both looking very serious. Let's have a drink.' They raised their glasses and chinked them as David proposed, 'To *Streetcar*.'

Inside, they ate a first course of trout with almonds. Philip had never eaten trout and he found it delicious, more subtle than the mackerel which his dad caught by the dozens in his nets at L'Etacq and then brought home to freeze. And he'd certainly never before had almonds with fish. They had spent some time reminiscing about *Twelfth Night*, and then David and Jane started discussing *Streetcar*. Philip didn't mind that he couldn't really participate; he loved listening to Jane and was intrigued by the vehemence with which she defended Blanche. She was sitting directly opposite him and he saw again the little red patch appear on her neck. He was entranced by the brightness of her eyes as she refused to let David's arguments go unchallenged. In the light from the table candles, her face seemed to glow. He wanted someone to paint her portrait and frame it for him to preserve her in this moment of bewitching beauty. David had argued that Stanley was also a sympathetic character, and Philip struggled to understand how David could defend a rapist. But he knew that David loved arguing so could simply have been playing devil's advocate.

He was left alone with Jane after he'd helped David clear away the plates and returned to the table, leaving David in the kitchen to attend to the final details of the main course.

'He can't believe what he was saying about Stanley, surely?' Jane protested before Philip had even sat back down.

'Who knows? But it seems to me that the play will be better if it's more complex than the goody versus the baddy, surely. I mean, think of Malvolio. Surely that bit of the play works because Feste, and especially Toby and Maria, become really nasty and cruel and the audience is invited to feel some sympathy for him?'

'Yes, I know that. In fact, apparently when the play was first performed, members of the audience stood up at one point in support of Stanley. If you knew the play you would no doubt argue that Blanche provokes him, but the simple fact is that he rapes her and that is inexcusable.'

He liked her passion. He looked at her and smiled.

'What?' she said.

'When you get heated there's this little patch of pink that appears on your neck.' And he pointed to the spot. She felt the place and as she did he saw her freshly shaved armpit. There was a small smooth patch of pencil-shade cross-hatching. She noticed he was looking and dropped her arm and rearranged the napkin on her lap.

David appeared with a large brown casserole pot for which Jane quickly created space on the table by moving wine glasses out of the way. He then went back out, reappearing immediately with a steaming bowl of broccoli that he placed alongside the casserole.

'Jane, help yourself. This is my Italian version of coq au vin. It's chicken with bacon lardons and celery in a sauce of marjoram and Marsala wine. And broccoli. I don't do potatoes.'

'Mmm. Smells good.' She helped herself to a very modest portion before passing the serving spoons to Philip.

'Please take more than Jane, Philip.'

'I intend to, don't worry.'

When David had served himself, he announced, 'I invited the two of you here as you know to talk about *Streetcar* and to plan a rehearsal schedule.' He reached behind himself to a bookcase on which he had placed a pen, a small pad and three copies of the play. 'Now, it's a long play and we have a very short rehearsal period. There's a cast of about a dozen, but we're going to double some of the minor characters. But most of the play is taken up by Blanche and Stanley – you two – and Stella and Mitch, that's Jenny and Peter Donaldson. What we need to do is agree some days when you two can basically rehearse all day. It will be intense and hard work but also great fun. Jenny and Peter will need to rehearse in seriously large chunks, too. I'm confident we can get it done – if you two, and Peter and Jenny, make sure you work incredibly hard and learn the lines as soon as possible.'

'Fine by me. I stopped working in the shop last week, so I can rehearse all day, every day if necessary.' Philip was envisaging spending long late summer days with Jane.

'Me, too, more or less. And I know Jenny is very keen, but when she's back at school she will only be able to manage evenings and weekends.'

'That's fine. I have to go back to school, too,' David said. 'It's much the same with Peter. OK, well that sounds good. I think the project is viable. That's exciting.'

David then proceeded to pass them the scripts and suggested they read the first encounter between Stanley and Blanche. He provided a bit of a synopsis for Philip, with Jane chipping in, and suggested they should read from Stanley's entrance in scene 1.

'American accents, presumably?' Jane asked.

'Of course.'

'Oh crikey, I'm not very good at accents,' Philip protested.

Jane stared at him. 'Don't be a wimp. Just do it.'

David read aloud the stage directions describing Stanley: *"Since earliest manhood the centre of his life has been pleasure with women, the giving and taking of it, not with weak indulgence but with the power and pride of a richly feathered male bird among hens."*

'It's good to know I'm going to be able to make use of my own personal experience to get into character,' Philip said. He dared himself to look at Jane. She held his gaze and smiled.

They reached the moment when Stanley takes off his shirt, and Philip immediately made a mental note to try to acquire some dumbbells. And then David suddenly screeched and Philip nearly jumped out of his seat before realising David was doing his impression of a cat being caught in a New Orleans street fight. David continued the sound effects by whistling what Philip assumed was the polka music the script required as Jane announced that Blanche was going to be sick.

'Well, I'll eat your pudding, then,' Philip offered, gallantly. And Jane smiled. Again. She then followed David out of the room, taking her own plate and Philip's, before returning to collect the broccoli dish and David's plate. When she returned, leaving David to prepare the pudding, she looked at the photograph on his bookcase. David was with a young woman on what she thought might be a cliff path on the north of the island.

'Philip, have you seen this?'

'Yes, that's David with his wife.'

'His wife? But he's not married.'

'No, he isn't. But he was. She died about five years ago. Complications in childbirth. The baby was stillborn. A boy, apparently.'

'Oh, that's terrible. I didn't know.'

David chose this very moment to reappear, with three glass bowls on a tray. 'Why do you two always look so serious? Do you not like each other or something? This will be a problem in rehearsals, you know?'

'I am prepared to ignore my real feelings for Jane for the sake of the play,' Philip offered, glaring at her. She glared back and twitched her nose in a way that thrilled him.

'Well, that's a relief,' said David. 'And this is zabaglione. Very slimming, Jane: egg yolks, Marsala wine and sugar.'

'Mmm, that's really nice,' Philip hummed.

'What about a first rehearsal on Monday at 9.30?' David asked. 'Just you two and Jenny. All your scenes together. For most of the day or until we're all too exhausted to carry on.'

It was agreed. Philip saw Jane was struggling with her zabaglione. 'Need some help with that, Jane?'

'Yes, please. Sorry, David, it's lovely but quite rich.'

'I'm sure Philip is happy to help out.'

She passed her dish across the table. Philip noticed she had left her spoon in the bowl and thought the imaginary book of etiquette he had consulted yesterday would dictate that he remove her spoon and use his own to eat from her bowl. But he wanted to touch her spoon, and put it in his mouth. It had been passed between her lips and placed on her tongue and then softly smoothed clean by her lips as she'd withdrawn it. He noticed her looking at him and thought she was reading his mind. She suddenly became Tess Durbeyfield, eating the strawberry proffered by Alec d'Urberville.

They had remained sitting at the dining table to read the penultimate scene, in which Stanley attacks Blanche. Philip was shocked by Stanley's brutality.

'Do you see what I mean now?' Jane demanded. 'It's unforgivable.'

'Does he believe it when he says, "*We've had this date with each other from the beginning*"?' Philip asked.

'Yes, I think he does,' David said. 'And what's more, I think she knows it too.'

They were on the way home, having thanked their host and complimented him on his cooking and having confirmed arrangements for Monday's rehearsal. They talked again just a little about David's wife and realised they didn't know her name. They agreed that David's insatiable appetite for putting on plays could partly be explained by the profound hole in his life her death must have left.

'I didn't think about it at the time,' Jane said, 'but do you remember – one of my lines in that first scene is "*The boy died*". What must David have been thinking then?'

'Oh God, yes. I think it must be very hard, though, you know, to understand fully what a parent's love for a child is like unless you are a parent. That's why I don't think I'll really appreciate *King Lear* until I'm about sixty.'

'Are you going to wait until then to become a parent?'

'No, of course not. Well, I hope not. But you know what I mean.'

The mood had become rather dark and they sat in silence for a minute or two.

'Does Jenny know the play?' Philip asked.

'Yes, she loves it too. But she wants to be Blanche rather than Stella so she's a bit jealous.' Jane was smiling.

'You could swap parts.'

'No, we certainly could not! I'm playing Blanche. And anyway, why do you say that?'

'It was just a thought.' She turned to look at him and he thought she knew what he meant.

It had been a long evening and it was late. The moonlit country lanes were deserted. He wanted her to stop the car so they could go for a walk together, and he looked at her beautiful profile wondering if he dared make the suggestion. But she then took him completely by surprise by slowing down and bringing the car to a standstill.

'Would you like to drive?'

'What do you mean?'

'Shall we swop places?'

'Are you serious?'

'I'm always serious, Philip. Where's your spirit of adventure? Don't be boring.'

'Jane, it would be illegal. I haven't passed my test, I've had too much to drink and I'm not insured. Apart from that, though, brilliant idea.'

'Wimp!' They stared at each other and in the darkness of the car he could see a bright spark in both of her eyes. She continued to stare at him. He looked at her mouth as she moistened her lips. He felt he was somehow being challenged, a challenge anyone who wanted to be with her needed to take on and to come through. He was still looking her in the eye, but she then looked down. Was she staring at his groin? She looked back up and he knew she was silently asking, 'Have you or have you not got it in you?'

He looked away, opened the passenger door, got out and walked round the back of the car to the driver's door. He opened it, and she hitched her dress a little higher and got out, smiling at him as she brushed past, ever so close. When they were both in their seats, she looked at him and said, 'Come on then. Know which pedal is which?'

'I must be mad. Almost as mad as you.' He put the car in gear and pulled away, surprisingly smoothly considering he'd never driven the vehicle before. He concentrated hard on the road even though all the while he could feel her looking at him. He twitched when a rabbit scuttled across the road in front of him.

'You're very good, Philip. I'm impressed. I could get used to this, being chauffeured around.'

'Don't get too comfortable. I'm not going much further. I'm going to pull in at the lay-by just past St John's church and it will be your turn again.'

He saw a squashed hedgehog on the road, its guts spilt out, and he felt a wave of fear and nausea making his flesh creep as he gripped the steering wheel even tighter. He was immensely relieved when he was able to pull over and he could stop holding his breath. He carefully placed the car in neutral, and then felt her hand on his. He looked at her smiling face.

'Just checking you weren't leaving it in gear, Philip.'

He wanted to pull her towards him. He wanted to kiss those lips, so recently moistened. He felt an almost overwhelming desire to hold her close so that she couldn't escape, so that she could no longer torment him with those damned eyes.

He turned away, roughly shoved open the car door and went round to her side. She was slowly getting out, apparently without a care and with all the time in the world. They resumed their proper seats. He thought he would show her exactly what spirit of adventure he had by putting his hand on hers when she put the car into gear, but he considered it for too long and the moment was lost. But he had proved he had the spirit, hadn't he? He certainly wasn't a wimp. He thought he could be a match for her and he thought she'd like that.

As she pulled out of the lay-by, she caught his eye and smiled. 'Not sure I'd want to go on a road trip across America with you, Philip; you wouldn't pull your weight.'

'The thing is, Jane, I'd love to go on a road trip with you and I'd do all the driving if that was what you wanted. But only when I've passed my test. And I'm not doing that again, so don't try to make me.'

'I won't ask. And you've already passed my test.' He had only just started to breathe normally again, but now she had quickened his pulse once more.

She pulled up outside his house. He thought again about trapping her hand as she put the car in neutral but knew he'd missed his chance; it needed to have happened earlier, if at all. He desperately didn't want the evening to end but knew it must. He opened the car door and turned back to her. 'Thank you very much for the lifts, Jane. I really enjoyed the evening. Apart from those insane three minutes. See you on Monday. *All good wishes.*' And he climbed out, closed the door and walked towards his house. He didn't know what had made him say the last three words but he was already regretting them.

LATE AUGUST 1976
JERSEY

'What else was I supposed to write? The card was being passed around the whole cast in a bit of a last-minute rush and I didn't have time to think of anything witty or more interesting.'

'I'm sorry. It's just me being neurotic. And unfair. Please forget I said it.'

'Not easy, Philip. But I'll try, if you forget I wrote it.'

'Not easy, Jane,' he echoed. He saw her jaw tighten. 'Sorry. That was silly and cheap. OK, let's just let it go. I will if you will.'

'I will,' she said, and he looked at her face and bizarrely imagined they were standing next to each other in church and she was wearing not her jeans and blouse but a white dress and a simple headdress of red roses. He briefly thought about taking her hand and miming putting on a ring, but the moment was wiped when David broke off his conversation with Jenny and said, 'Thank you, Jane. That's actually you done for today. It's Stanley and Stella now for the rest of the afternoon. Go and learn some lines.'

'I'd like to watch for a bit, but then I'll go and sit under a tree somewhere to learn lines before coming back to take my little sister home.' Philip glanced at Jenny and caught the look of irritation on her face.

'Stay as long as you like, my dear, but you must learn the lines.'

'I will. Don't worry.'

It was more than a week after the supper at David's and Philip's Parthian shot, and the remark had simmered away unspoken of during the rehearsals that followed, but Jane had chosen to confront him today, embarrassed and confused rather than angry, and clearly tired. He had wanted to say something the next time they'd met and on every other occasion after that but couldn't actually be certain that she had registered the comment or understood it, though his instincts told him there was something hanging in the air between them. But it was out in the open now and he hoped they could move on.

They were now rehearsing the intimate section near the end of scene three, the Marlon Brando bit, as they called it, where a contrite Stanley emerges from the cold shower his mates have forced him into and screams for his wife to return to him from a friend's apartment upstairs to where she has retreated when Stanley struck her in a moment of drunken madness. Philip didn't know if he was pleased or not that Jane was sitting in the auditorium, ready to watch.

'Stell-lahhhhh!' Philip screams with what he intends to be the 'heaven-splitting violence' demanded in the stage directions. Jenny walks slowly down the stairs. For a moment, Philip recalls seeing Jenny descend from the deck above on the boat. And he thinks of her sister, sitting in the audience. They stare at each other and then embrace. He knows that they are both supposed to be emitting 'low, animal moans', but he manages only a brief, whimpery exhalation before falling to his knees. He then presses his face to her belly, and it is unavoidably the lower part, and he realises his left hand is on her bottom. He feels her hands on his head as she raises him to his feet. He places his right arm around her back and bends his knees so that he can put his left arm behind her knees. He scoops her up, and her face is so close to his and he forces himself to stay looking into her eyes. He can feel her breath. He is determined to make it seem like he isn't finding her incredibly heavy, not to be polite to her but to impress the audience, and he carries her to the bed. He can't work out the mechanics required to put her down gracefully, and, feeling the veins in his neck bulging, he lets go of her legs and she manages somehow to end up on the bed. He knows he should really lie on top of her, but this is the first time they've done the scene, so he decides to go down on his knees beside the bed and place his head on her shoulder. Not the final moment of erotic intensity Mr Williams envisaged, he realises, but it will have to do for now. He holds the tableau for a few seconds and then turns round, ostensibly to seek David's thoughts, but actually in a desperate desire to see Jane's response. But she is no longer there.

'Well done, you two,' David said. 'I almost believed that. Right, I have something I need to do in the common room; A levels fall-out, unfortunately. I'll be five minutes, ten at most. So you can have a well-deserved break. We'll do scene 2 when I get back.'

Jenny was now sitting on the bed and Philip sat alongside her. He was breathing deeply and noticed her smell. Similar to Jane – nice, but somehow heavier and a little sharper.

'Sorry about any errant hands, Jenny.'

'Oh, don't worry about that. As I'm sure you know, they should really be much more errant.'

'The actor's usual problem of not knowing what to do with your hands, but magnified somewhat.'

'Except that you *do* know what to do with them, but it's hard to do it. It would be much easier if Jane were playing Stella, wouldn't it?'

'Even harder, actually.' He had responded before thinking through what she was saying. And her follow-up put him on the spot.

'Really? Why?' He looked at her and saw that she wanted to talk about him and Jane. Why? Had she spoken to her sister about him? Had Jane asked her to say anything? He decided he would risk inviting her confidence.

'Why do you think?'

'I can't imagine, Philip. It's just acting, isn't it?' He saw a sparkle in her eyes. Eyes like Jane's. He could see she was very pretty, beautiful in fact, but he felt no sexual attraction. He enjoyed her company because she was her sister's sister and because she was precociously intelligent and mature beyond her years. *And what have she and Jane been saying to each other?* He couldn't think of a risk-free way of trying to say or find out more.

'Yes, it's just acting, Jenny. And one should never confuse acting with real life. Not *"all the world's a stage"*, after all.'

They looked at each other and smiled and a satisfyingly weary silence ensued. But then Jenny got up off the bed and walked to her bag, from which she took a bottle of water. She drank from it, and then offered it to Philip. He shook his head, so she bent down to put it back in her bag.

'She likes you, you know.' He stared at her back, and then she turned round and met his look.

He could feel himself starting to blush. 'She's told you this, has she?'

'Yes. Well, not as such, but we've talked about you and it's pretty obvious.'

'How is it obvious?'

'She talks about things you've said and done and the way you look at her and she obviously enjoys it. She loves your hair.'

'Has she said that?'

'Yes, she *has* said that, I promise.' Philip found himself running his fingers through his hair and wanting a mirror to look in. He loved her dark brown hair; why should she not like his blond mop? He remembered he'd washed it last night and wondered if she had smelt it while they were rehearsing earlier.

'Go on, ask her out. You've got nothing to lose.'

I've got everything to lose. She is the only really important thing in my life.

'Mmm,' he said. 'I'll think about it.'

'Time and tide and my sister... But be careful, Philip. She likes getting her own way. Don't let her bully you.'

David reappeared, looking a little flustered. *Difficult parents, probably,* Philip thought. 'Come on then, stop being idle, from the top of scene 2, please,' David instructed, and his command was dutifully obeyed.

An hour later, when they stopped rehearsing the scene, Philip realised he had not noted in his scripts any of the new blocking and everything they'd done was just a very vague memory. He had spent much of the scene inviting Jane out – for a drink, for a meal, for a walk on the cliffs or on the beach. He had taken her home to his mum's house and they'd sat in the garden after he'd made her a cup of tea. She had been wearing jeans cut off to make shorts, blue espadrilles and a brilliant white sleeveless blouse. He'd sat down very close to her and she'd run her hand through his hair. He had slowly leant forward to kiss her, and she hadn't moved away.

'OK. Not bad, you two,' David sighed. 'Well done. But we're all getting a little tired, aren't we? It's not quite five, but I think we should stop. That's been a very full day and a very good one, too.'

Jenny started packing her bag, and David collected his bits and pieces from the table at the back of the auditorium, and then they all walked slowly out of the building to be almost blinded by the dazzling sunshine. Jane was heading towards them, basket in one hand and script in the other. Philip smiled at her. 'Had a nice nap in the sun?' he asked.

'Certainly not. I spread my blanket out under a tree and did exactly as David instructed.'

'Not like you to do as you're told, Jane,' David said.

'Mum would agree with that sentiment,' Jenny added. Philip saw Jane try to ignore her sister's barb. He thought Jenny would be getting an earful in the car on the way home.

He smiled at Jane and dared himself to run his hand through his hair. He saw Jenny also smiling at her. Jane was now looking bemused. He was savouring a rare moment: for once he felt like he had the upper hand.

But now was obviously not the time. There was no rush.

He would wait until after tomorrow's rehearsal. He'd have to prepare the script tonight.

They were coming towards the end of the next day's intense, six-hour session. His scenes with Jane had gone well. They trusted each other and enjoyed seeing the sparks fly. In the best possible way they had been competing with each other, both as Stanley and Blanche, and as actors. The room had been a sweaty and genuinely creative hive of activity, fine beads of sweat even appearing on Jane's forehead just below her hairline and above her upper lip. Philip wondered what they would taste like. He wished he'd had the presence of mind to take along a spare T-shirt; he'd remember next time.

He was watching the last few minutes of rehearsal. It was a Blanche and Mitch scene, at the end of which they were going to kiss. He was quite impressed with Peter, who seemed to have just the right kind of gentle stodginess for Mitch. The moment of the kiss arrived and Philip saw Jane look at him for the smallest of split seconds before she kissed Peter. Philip was breathing slowly. It should be a long, gentle kiss full of yearning, but he saw Jane ease herself out of it and turn her face downstage so that she could look at him in the auditorium as she said, "*Sometimes – there's God – so quickly*." Philip could see from her face that she was thinking exactly the same as him. They were both remembering the kiss in *Twelfth Night* and how she had emerged from it and stared defiantly at Philip. Now she was looking at him, a look of apology on her face, he thought. Philip imagined, too, that she was thinking, *I wish that had been you.* He looked at Peter and briefly felt an irrational deep hatred. He hardly knew Jane and he had already kissed her, whereas Philip had been worshipping her for two years and hadn't even touched her in real life. He noticed how Jane had suddenly become very becalmed, while

Peter was sneaking a look at his watch. *That meant nothing to him*, he thought. He reminded himself of Jenny's words: 'It's just acting.'

But his time had come, and he knew what he was going to do. He had taken Jane's straw hat from her bag and had hidden it by the door into the theatre. They all helped to tidy things away and to put rubbish in the bins and had gathered up their stuff. They'd said goodbyes and Peter was rushing off on his bike and David was walking with Jane towards their cars parked under the clock tower. Philip had waited by the theatre door and allowed them to go ahead. David was already in his car and Jane was about to get into hers when he called out her name. She looked towards him and he waved her hat at her. She clearly expected him to walk towards her, but he didn't move so she made her way back to him. He pretended to snatch it away from her just as she was about to take it but then handed it over. She managed a tired smile and a weary sigh as she put it on.

'Jane?'

'Yes, Philip?'

'Would you like to go for a drink sometime, or maybe a walk, or maybe both? I'm versatile.'

She smiled. A tired smile again, but it was warm and gentle.

'Yes, I would, Philip. I think I'd enjoy that very much. And I'm versatile, too.' He smiled at her. A wonky smile, he suspected. And he was burning and purring and aching with happiness. She took hold of both of his hands and looked into his eyes. He could barely breathe. She paused before continuing: 'But, Philip, it will just be a drink and a walk. I don't want it to be anything else.' He thought he must have misheard. But she continued: 'I like you so much and I love being with you.' She paused once more, and he thought again that he had misheard. But then she carried on: 'But in a fortnight you'll be going to Birmingham. And what then? It's just not sensible to start something now.'

'But I'll be back for Christmas.'

'I know, and we'll see each other again then, I promise. I'll miss you very much next term. And then after Christmas I'm going to be doing my course in Italy. You must admit, it wouldn't exactly be great timing, would it?'

He could see the logic; it wasn't difficult. He was starting to feel a sense of panic. He wanted to tell her he loved her and he didn't want to live without her. But he knew as well as she did that they couldn't be together. He felt a huge cave forming in his stomach and was working so hard to stop becoming visible the tears that were pricking behind his eyes. He wanted to hold her tight and then refuse to let her go, but he stood there, immobile. He looked at her hands holding his. He loved her hands. He wanted to hold them forever. He looked up again and saw her face, her beautiful face, turned up towards him, tilted in an attempt to ask him if he understood. He saw her eyes. Were there perhaps some tears forming in hers too?

She let go of his hands, stretched up to kiss him on the cheek and then turned to hurry back to her car. He watched her drive away and thought he would be unhappy for the rest of his life.

7

AUGUST 2018

WORCESTER

He thought he would head for the cathedral, sneak in and try to see her in rehearsal but remain unseen. Only after he had passed a pupil walking in the opposite direction did he realise he had unwittingly ignored her friendly greeting. He turned round and smiled and apologised and waved and then thought his behaviour must have seemed rather strange to her.

The cathedral looked immense and majestic, its beauty startling against the cloudless blue sky. He thought of the regular debate he had with his friend, Andy, and how Andy was always more moved by nature, by mountains, and he was more moved by man-made things. Like cathedrals. This cathedral now, looking down protectively on its city, its ancient stones having endured centuries of history, having witnessed thousands of baptisms and funerals, and having heard and absorbed the words of thousands of couples swearing to love each other until death. It was now as it must surely have been forty years ago, he thought. Had it changed in any visible way? Did any of its floor flagstones look any different from forty years ago? *'So light a foot will ne'er wear out the everlasting flint.'* Had the wood of the pews changed colour at all? How much had he changed in forty years? And what about her? What had he learnt from a full career and half a lifetime about his feelings? How could he still feel so intensely and with such excitement about someone he hadn't seen since she said goodbye and walked out of the departures hall at the airport on September 30th, 1977. She had given him a copy of John Fowles's *The Collector,* 'With all my love' inscribed on the inside cover. He remembered how hurtful the words had been because they were clearly not true. His throat had hurt and he had felt the bile rising as she walked away from him, compelled to accept that the summer they had just shared was over, as was the relationship. She would head off to her first year at Durham fancy-free whereas he would return for his second year at Birmingham utterly miserable, not knowing what had gone wrong, why for her it had run its course.

He found himself in the cathedral's north porch, nodded to and smiled at a familiar canon, and edged towards the nave, to a position alongside a pillar from where he could see the choir on its raised platform. They were rehearsing the Mozart Requiem. He thought he recognised the conductor – perhaps he'd seen him on TV – and here he was now conducting the BBC Singers and Jane would be following his every move. *He must now have her complete attention,* Philip thought, and he felt a sharp stab of jealousy. Not that he could actually see where she was. He remembered how a few years earlier he had been watching a concert on television and the camera was panning across the faces of the singers, all absolutely focussed and oblivious of everything except the music. His heart had thumped into his ribs when she appeared on the screen. She was only there for a second, but he had been sure it was her. *It could easily be, couldn't it?* he had told himself.

She was a singer, after all. He had remembered going to see her singing in *Dido and Aeneas*. He remembered her singing 'Summertime' when they were in the car that summer. How could a human voice be so effortlessly beautiful? Was there ever a more gorgeous melody? How special was it to be the only member of the audience at this impromptu concert? He had wondered: *Can I ever be as happy as this again?*

Of course it was her. His breathing had become stupidly fast and shallow. Pan back the other way, he had silently commanded the TV director. *Nobody is interested in all those tenors. Just show me her one more time so I can be sure. Lower, lower. No! Who wants to see the conductor, for heaven's sake? My God, it is her. A close-up. Her eyes! Her mouth. Her mouth. She's still there. The director is falling in love with her too. She has stolen the whole show.* And then she was gone. And she hadn't reappeared again for the rest of the concert.

Philip was jolted out of his reverie when the singing stopped abruptly and the vast edifice was suddenly eerily quiet. The conductor was then rather short with his choir, saying that some of them had made the same mistake again, and insisting they sing a particular passage once more to get it right if they wanted the rehearsal to finish on time. Well over one hundred adults accepting in shame-faced silence and without question the opinion of a young man in a silly Hawaiian shirt and with a little stick in his hand. *Don't you dare make her late,* Philip thought. He still hadn't spotted her; didn't actually have the best of angles. But he didn't want her to see him looking for her. A bit too eager. And then suddenly there she was! He'd found her! Yes, hanging on the conductor's every word. He remembered another occasion when he had been looking for her and he left the cathedral by the north door and headed for the river at the west end. Leaning on the wall overlooking the river, Philip thought about the occasion he had met her in Florence on the Ponte Vecchio.

8

APRIL 1977

FLORENCE

He hadn't wanted to go to Italy with David, but the thought of meeting Jane in Florence and then being able to return home together was impossible to resist. He had completed two terms at university and had spent longer on his letters to her back home than on most of his essays. Even so, university life was good: he had made good friends, including someone who clearly wanted to be a girlfriend, and had auditioned successfully for the Italian Society's production of Pirandello's *Right You Are, If You Think So*. He remembered how for a while he'd pretended to his new mates in hall that it was going to be performed in Italian. He had drunk too much beer and not eaten particularly well, but he was a student, after all.

He had agreed to go with David to Italy over Easter, chiefly to plan the summer production of *Macbeth*, in which he and Jane would play the gruesome twosome.

He was in David's white Toyota Celica approaching Florence. David was a reluctant and dreadful driver, so Philip had driven most of the way from St Malo, for three long days. He had been relieved that the sea crossing from Jersey had been very smooth and he had been able to read without worrying about retaining his breakfast. As they approached Florence, the prospect of seeing the Duomo was as nothing compared to the prospect of seeing Jane on the Ponte Vecchio.

She was in Florence doing a history of art course during part of her year off before starting at Durham. Philip felt a little anxious that his knowledge of renaissance art was embarrassingly deficient, but he thought an enthusiasm to learn would be as engaging as any expertise and he knew full well that most people like to be able to exhibit their new knowledge and to illustrate their cultural superiority. She had written to him regularly since the start of her course in February and though he had tormented himself by trying to read things between her lines that probably weren't there, he hoped she had not formed any close attachment with anyone else on the course. But he felt certain that she would have attracted someone's interest. He remembered how he had been on a course at Villiers Park two years before to help prepare for English A Level and one of the girls there had been of more interest to most of the boys on the course than *King Lear* and *The Clerk's Tale*. She had actually looked a little like Jane: dark eyed; more mischievous but less mysterious.

Italian drivers were conforming to their image and reputation. There were long queues on the road running alongside the Arno and many of the locals had got out of their cars and were gesticulating through 360 degrees while keeping one hand on the horn. A traffic jam was not what was required. He thought about abandoning the vehicle with David and running to the bridge. The thought of being late for what was a ridiculously improbable but unbelievably exciting rendezvous filled him with anxiety.

But slowly the traffic moved forward and at last the famous bridge came into view. Would she show up? Was she already there? Was this the most important meeting of her life as well? What if her class had overrun? Had he got the day right? The time right? Would it be so crowded he wouldn't be able to find her?

Just fifty yards past the bridge he was able to pull over and leave David to look after the car. The timing was perfect: it was 3.55pm. He had time to walk back to the bridge trying to compose himself, savouring those few minutes when he could anticipate the ecstasy of seeing her. He tried to walk casually, but his heart was beating so fast and he could feel it pumping in his neck. He was in one of the most famous cities in the world, approaching one of the world's most celebrated landmarks, but he had only one picture in his mind and he felt that this was the stuff of fiction, except it was real, and he was the protagonist.

Was she there? Would he see her before she saw him? He turned onto the bridge. He took no notice of the shops, the jewellers and locksmiths on either side. On which side would she be? Would she have worked out from which side he would come? Towards the middle to be safe? He saw her, and noticed immediately her bohemian skirt and her basket. Her eyes were so bright. That expression could only mean she was excited, too. He rushed to her and then found himself embracing her fiercely. He hadn't thought about this; it had just happened. And she held him too. He had never held her before. She felt small and precious. He felt as though he was protecting her and he thought she wanted his protection in this place far away from home. He noticed her perfume – it was Charlie, he knew. As they came out of the hold he saw her face, her smile, and he smelt her – not the perfume, but the smell of her, her hair, her clothes, her skin – and felt profound happiness, an intensity of emotion he had never before experienced. He wanted to kiss her. He always wanted to kiss her. Those lips. What would she taste like? But she started to talk…

'That was good timing. Bang on four o'clock.'

'I wouldn't have wanted to miss that hug.' He was surprised he had been able to speak.

'Me neither.'

They smiled, and Philip replayed her last two words over and over in his head as they walked towards the car. 'Me neither.' That's what she said. 'Me neither.' She wanted to be hugged. She'd hugged him back. Her eyes were smiling. He'd seen them. He should have kissed her. *Oh, God, why didn't I kiss her? She would have let me, wouldn't she? Maybe that was what she had wanted, too.*

9

AUGUST 2018

SATURDAY
WORCESTER

He was enjoying the lulling sound of the oars caressing the water and the beautiful synchronicity of the blades, but Philip turned away from the two different quads smoothly making their way up the river and saw a slow stream of people emerging from the cathedral's north porch. Determined to appear casual, he put his hands in his trouser pockets and strolled towards them. *No sight of her yet. I hope she knows her north from her south.*

She does. She smiled as she spotted him. Philip felt the smile looked completely genuine and he managed what he knew was a lopsided smile back.

'I don't know Worcester very well – only been here thirty-five years. But there's a Costa down the High Street. Are you happy with that?'

'That's fine. I'd be happy anywhere.'

They crossed into Cathedral Plaza. For a brief moment he considered taking her hand, but he didn't. He remembered holding her hand at the *Macbeth* curtain call. Forty years ago. He glanced down at his shirt to check if any sweat patches had started to appear and suddenly felt he couldn't think of a single thing to talk about.

She rescued him – again: 'That rehearsal was dull, but I suppose it had to be done. There are some tricky bits in the Dies Irae we needed to sort out. It was the tenors' fault. Anyway.' She exhaled and then inhaled deeply. 'What a beautiful day!'

'Outside or in?'

'Oh, inside I think,' she said, and he readily agreed, conscious that he had less chance of being noticed inside and less chance of overheating. And then he thought how mad it was to imagine he was doing anything wrong, having coffee with an old friend.

There was a table tucked away at the back. He wanted this to be happening in a nicer place. A café in Rome, a bar in Florence or a beachside café in Jersey.

'Go on, you sit down. Earl Grey?'

'You remembered!'

'Of course. Anything else? Large caramel shortbread, a couple of brownies?' He knew perfectly well she would never touch such things. She shook her head and smiled. Again!

Philip waited impatiently while the young chap behind the bar pushed buttons on a machine that gurgled and hissed and produced for him a cup of tea and an Americano, both perched ludicrously off-centre on their ridiculous saucers. He carried them carefully to the table.

He sat down and said, '"*Do not laugh at me, for as I am a man I think this lady to be my friend, Jane.*"' Jane looked at him quizzically. '*King Lear*,' he said. 'He's just woken up and sees the daughter he thought he would never see again. And he can't believe it. Except *he* thinks he's in hell.' Jane momentarily looked away, a serious expression on her face. *A troubled look, almost,* Philip thought. But then she turned back.

'She's not called Jane. And how long have I got before they hang me?'

'Don't worry – I won't let them. Well, come on then, you'd better tell me what you've been doing for the last forty years. What time is your concert?'

She smiled. Yet again. 'I'll keep it brief.'

And she described a full life of singing, teaching singing, of married life and being a mother and of living in Highgate.

'Highgate, really! One of our boys lives quite close, in Kentish Town. I'm surprised we haven't bumped into each other in the street or on the tube when I've been down there. Are you in any of the gangs? A Shark or a Jet?'

'I failed the audition.'

'I failed lots of them so became a teacher.'

'Those who can… those who can't—'

'Except we both know that's rubbish, don't we?' He realised he hadn't had a single sip of coffee, so drank some and was surprised it was still hot. Jane had almost finished her tea. 'So, tell me more about your husband and daughter.'

'Annie, my daughter, did history of art at UCL and then a PhD at the Courtauld Institute. She works at the V and A. Had a bit of disaster with her marriage, unfortunately, and spends as much time with me as she does at her home in Clapham.' She leant her chin upon her hand, her fingers lightly pressed against her face, and momentarily stared at her empty cup. '*O, that I were a glove upon that hand that I might touch that cheek.*'

She looked up, straight at him. 'Bill is so busy and often works very late. Sorry, Bill is my husband. Bill King. He's a partner at a corporate law firm in the city. When they are completing a deal he can sometimes be at work all or much of the night. And when he does finish at a reasonable hour he's so tired and irritable when he comes home.' Philip thought she seemed to realise she hadn't needed to say so much. 'But he earns an obscene amount and we have a very comfortable lifestyle, so the hard work and long hours do bring some rewards.' Philip imagined she was going to continue, and she looked as though she had more to say. But she didn't.

She looked at him again and Philip felt some concern when he saw what he thought was sadness in her eyes before she smiled again, not quite convincingly. The quiet moment was broken as a young woman tried to park her pushchair in a space that wasn't big enough and bumped it into Philip's chair.

'Sorry, love.'

He shook his head and smiled at her: 'Don't worry.'

'Your turn,' Jane said.

'Pardon?'

'What have you been up to since 1977? The concert starts in about six hours.' She smiled again, this time a smile that he saw lifted her cheekbones and did reach her eyes.

'Well, I have a wife, Laura. We've been married for thirty-four years. She works in environmental health, in Malvern, which is about six miles over that way,' and he pointed in what he thought was the right direction. 'We have thirty-year-old twin sons. Tom is a solicitor in London and is married to a lovely girl he met at university; she's a physiotherapist. Oh, yes, he's the one who lives in Kentish Town. And George plays rugby for London Irish. He lives in Brixton with his girlfriend, who works for Sky.'

'Twins! Carrying and giving birth to one is hard enough. And looking after two babies. Your poor wife. How did you manage?'

Philip immediately looked down at his coffee. 'Not sure. I can't really remember very much. You'd have to ask Laura.'

He sipped his coffee and stared briefly at the woman with the pushchair. He wanted to change the subject. 'What are you doing after the concert?' he asked as casually as he could.

'I'm catching the last train back to London. From Foregate Street, 21.20, I think.'

'What time does the concert finish? Is there time for a drink before the train?'

'Yes. Maybe an hour or so. Definitely time.'

'Well, if you like, I could meet you outside the cathedral and we could go to a pub on the way to the station. There are plenty down the high street.'

'I'd like that. I really would, Philip.'

He felt a sudden buzz of excitement: she'd said his name, in the way she'd sometimes said it forty years ago when it had thrilled him so much. They left the café and walked back to the cathedral, and Philip said he ought to be getting home. Jane said she wanted to go back to her hotel to rest and have a bath and to change and have a light meal before the concert with a few of her fellow singers. Philip wanted to hug her with the intensity he had felt all those years earlier on the Ponte Vecchio but instead took her shoulders and pecked her on the cheek. He recollected a time she had stretched to kiss him on the cheek and he had wanted the world to end.

'Hope the concert goes well, and see you later.'

'Thank you. Looking forward to it. Looking forward to seeing you again, Philip.' And she reached out to take his hands, and squeezed them briefly before passing them back, all the while looking at him, her eyes smiling and tempting him to think they were offering the promise of intimacy.

Philip strode off, thinking it would be much cooler not to look back, desperate though he was for another sight of her. He had smelt her again and he had felt his skin tingle with pleasure and desire and his throat constrict with yearning and apprehension. And she had held his hands in hers. Fondly. More than that.

Some of the food stalls on the green had started to pack up, but he could still catch the aromas of freshly baked breads and various exotic spices he couldn't identify. A work colleague he wasn't particularly inclined to chat with was just emerging from the Common Room and was heading towards him, so he quickly got into his car and drove under the arch and started his journey home.

He tried to examine his feelings. He knew that nothing could happen with Jane. He would not change what he had with Laura, what he had shared for over thirty years. He had always been baffled by the reckless choices some people made which jeopardised everything they had built and nurtured just for some brief moments of adventure. But he also envied those who were less dull than him; those people whose story could conceivably be turned into exciting fiction. Nobody would ever write a play in which he featured, but if someone did, nobody would ever go to see it or talk passionately about it. Who could possibly find Lady Macduff more interesting than Lady Macbeth? Mercy Chant more lovable than Tess? Who would you prefer to be, Romeo or Benvolio?

'You've been a long time,' Laura said as he walked through the front door.

'Yes, sorry. Pottered around the stalls on College Green. I also bumped into this friend from schooldays. She's singing in a concert in the cathedral tonight. I don't think it's sold out – would you like to go?'

'What are they singing?'

'The Mozart Requiem.'

'Can't say I'm mad keen. In fact I can't go. Just remembered – I've signed up for the aqua aerobics class which starts at eight.'

'OK, but do you mind if I go?'

'Course not. What time will it finish? And what will we do about food?'

'Not sure, but it starts at seven. I did buy some chicken, but maybe we can make do with cheese and some fruit. We've got plenty of those nice chilli biscuits, I think.'

'That's fine.'

He didn't feel comfortable about not having told Laura who the friend was. 'Yes, I bumped into Jane on the Green. We were in a couple of plays together forty years ago and incredibly I haven't seen her since. I said I'd try to get to the concert and have a quick drink with her before she catches the train back to London tonight.'

'Well, that will be nice. Oh, by the way, Tom rang to say he has to go to Barcelona next month for work, and he's quite excited about that. Said he might be able to get to the Nou Camp. And George texted to say he was getting ready for a busy weekend at Dan's stag do. He assured me it would be a very civilised affair – poetry readings, walks in the countryside and maybe a glass of sherry before a light supper.'

'Yes, I'm sure. So, they're both OK?'

'Absolutely fine. Full of it. Oh, will you put the whirly line out for me please and hang out the washing?'

Philip was happy to do so. As he carried the line from the shed and across the patio to the familiar place on the lawn, he thought how lucky he was to have such a comfortable home and such a lovely garden that he and Laura had worked so hard on together over the twenty-five years they had been living there. It was looking beautiful in the August sunshine, and hanging up the washing wasn't a chore but a simple pleasure and an opportunity quietly to reflect on his happiness and to consider again the modest success he had made of his life. OK, he hadn't changed the world or made a fortune, and still hadn't written his novel, but life was good. The melancholic mood he'd been in earlier had disappeared. A good life, even if it was unremarkable. *Just be grateful,* he told himself. All the washing pegged up, he strolled to the bottom of the garden and sat on one of the chairs on the circular patio. The bay tree looked spectacularly healthy and the cherry tree that he had thought he might take out several years earlier because it had been so slow to grow was a beautiful shape and looked happy and vigorous; Laura had been right to insist they leave it alone. The lawn had survived what had been a hot summer so far and still looked green, partly because it was time to give it another cut.

'Would you like a little coffee?' Laura called from the French doors.

'Ooh. Yes, please.'

He told himself not to be ridiculous. *Go for a drink with Jane, enjoy reminiscing by all means and then come back here and be very grateful for everything you have. Don't throw this away.*

A couple of minutes later, they were sitting together, sipping a Nespresso lungo from their favourite ceramic cups bought on holiday in Crete.

'We're very lucky, aren't we?' he said, even though he was staring at the camellia that was one of the few disappointing plants in their garden.

Laura nodded slowly and he knew she understood what he was thinking about – their home, their careers, their life together and especially their two boys, Tom and George, high achievers both, both nicely settled with good prospects, lovely partners and an ingrained sense of right and wrong. She appeared about to voice her agreement when there was a tremendous noise as some kind of jet flew over the garden – very fast, very low and incredibly loud. He thought it was on an exercise from its airbase somewhere in Herefordshire, though he didn't really know why he was making this assumption. *What, all my pretty chickens and their dam in one fell swoop?* The line just dropped into Philip's mind and suddenly his spirits sank again. He got up and said, 'I think I'll mow the lawn.'

Some hours later, lawn striped, edges cut, some dead-heading done and Philip showered, they agreed that Laura was likely to be home first but that she shouldn't wait for Philip to eat. He had tried on several shirts and a number of pairs of trousers before deciding he looked slimmest in a pair of blue linen trousers and a pale grey shirt that wasn't too tight. He remembered the extraordinary clothes he had worn forty years earlier: the green velvet jacket, the trendy striped brown shirt with the white collar, the massive flares, and the completely bizarre shoes with absurd platform heels. He was pleased not to be dressing like that, but he wished he were as slim as he had been then when he hadn't thought at all about holding in his stomach. He smiled nostalgically when he noticed he did still have a bottle of Aramis which he used occasionally, his favourite scent back then, but he decided on a couple of short sprays of Sauvage, remembering that his older brother had always used Eau Sauvage when getting ready for what today's young people would call a BNO. He remembered that before he'd graduated to Aramis, he'd used either Brut, as advertised by Henry Cooper on the TV when he 'splashed it all over', or Cougar, a bottle of which he had been very happy to receive one Christmas. He remembered how he had at first borrowed his dad's razor and brush, and the mess he sometimes made of his face, and then how much the aftershave would sting. He winced at the memory of such teenage awkwardness and angst but could also remember how alive he had felt, how exciting it was to be going out and also how nervous he was. He smiled but also felt apprehensive when he realised he was feeling a similar excitement now, and he was grateful that he had not had to manoeuvre the razor today around any spots.

'You look nice,' Laura said. 'I've always liked that shirt.' And she straightened a collar that didn't need straightening and patted him on the chest. 'Have a good time. Resist the urge to sing along, please.' She smiled and they kissed briefly, and she stood watching him as he made his way to the car, and she waved as he drove off.

He parked on the Green, glanced briefly in the vanity mirror and wasn't too disheartened. He flipped the sun visor back into place. As he strolled towards the entrance into the cloisters he saw Tim, a former colleague, and they exchanged 'expert' assessments of the test match, agreeing that England should go on to win it. Neither seemed concerned to seek different company, so they found themselves sitting together halfway back on the pulpit side.

All the while, Philip was looking at Jane, mildly disappointed that she didn't seem to be scanning the audience to find him. But then the conductor made his entrance to enthusiastic applause, and Philip smiled, as he always did, at the idea that someone should be applauded before he'd started his work. He didn't remember many of his lessons starting with generous applause. Or ending with it.

The concert was wonderful, but Philip found his mind wandering even if his eyes didn't. Tim's frequent and regular little sniffs became very irritating. Philip was reminded of the occasion in Rome when he and Jane had been at a performance of Bizet's *Carmen* and Jane had had a terrible time trying, but failing, to avoid coughing. He remembered feeling so desperately sorry for her in her discomfort and embarrassment, whereas he only felt annoyed with Tim. He also remembered the expensive and frustrating mistake he and Jane had made in Rome, when they turned up at the ballet, excited at the prospect of seeing Nureyev dance, only to see the audience coming out of the opera house. Another look at the tickets had revealed the starting time was 18.30, not 8.30pm. He'd had another embarrassing experience at the theatre in Stratford. On a school trip, he and his mates had had a liquid lunch at The Dirty Duck before the matinee of *The Winter's Tale*, and for most of the very long first half he had thought of nothing except how desperate he was for the interval so he could get to the gents. And what a wildly improbable plot, he'd thought.

He felt mildly ashamed of his rather abrupt 'Goodnight, Tim' soon after the applause had stopped, but he was anxious to get to the north entrance, even though he knew full well the choir would not be leaving before the audience. And he was rather caught off guard when Jane appeared almost immediately; he hadn't thought about or rehearsed what he would say to her. But he found himself saying, 'Let's go for a drink at The Diglis,' and they headed towards the towpath. Jane put her arm through his, taking him completely by surprise. But he felt he didn't change his stride pattern and a couple of discreet deep breaths helped him appear relaxed, he hoped.

'I know this makes your walk to the station a little longer, but The Diglis is very nice and it's still very warm so we can sit outside.'

'Sounds perfect. Lead on, Macduff.'

'It's "*Lay on*", Jane, as I'm sure you must know.' Philip bit his tongue, but it was too late: he'd corrected her. She didn't seem remotely put out, but he still couldn't help seeing again the flush on her neck at the *Twelfth Night* rehearsal forty years earlier. He quickly tried to change the subject. 'I love the Lacrimosa. Imagine composing the music for your own funeral.'

'Most of the Lacrimosa was composed by someone else; Mozart died before he'd finished it. Apparently he only managed the first few bars.'

'Sounds like me on a pub crawl.'

Jane smiled and elbowed him gently in the ribs. She was perfectly happy to let Philip have the last word, he thought, having more than recovered the ground she'd lost by misquoting from *Macbeth*.

They'd arrived at the pub and Philip suggested Jane go through the lounge to get a table outside while he ordered the drinks. He stood at the bar and caught sight of himself in the mirrored wall behind the bottles and all the optics. Sixty years old. He wanted to be nineteen again.

'Sorry, yes, two glasses of dry white wine, please.' He saw the barman pour the wine into measuring cups and thought, *What's the point if you fill them so that they overflow?* But it wasn't remotely important.

'Cheers.'

'Thank you. Yes, cheers. What a beautiful evening. This is a lovely spot.'

'Yes, we come here quite often in the summer. Specially straight after work for an early evening drink.' She smiled warmly at him. 'I really enjoyed the concert. It must be great fun singing in a big choir. But it must be quite a commitment; I mean, it's a long way to come for one concert.'

'To be honest, I like trips like this. It's good to get out of London, even for a short while. Good to get away from things.'

'Well, you're welcome to come to Worcester whenever you want.' He knew that his remark wasn't quite appropriate, but he continued all the same: 'Even if you don't have a concert.' Jane stared at him and smiled, and he wanted to know what she was thinking.

He changed direction: 'What time will you get back home?'

'About midnight. I'll sleep on the train, I expect, even though I'll try to read.' She paused, but then looked up and added, 'Bill's away on business until the middle of next week, so the house will be empty.'

Philip thought of offering her accommodation for the night and driving her to London the next day but knew the idea was absurd. Instead, all he could manage was, 'Sorry.'

'It's hardly your fault! I choose to sing in the choir and I chose a lawyer for my husband.' Philip thought he detected regret in her tone. He felt sorry for her but then realised he was probably wilfully misreading her. But there was sadness in her eyes. She looked down and then back up at him, and he was reminded of the doey-eyed look of Princess Diana in the *Panorama* interview, and briefly wondered if Jane was playing with him in some way. He knew he would be powerless to resist, chiefly because he wouldn't want to.

He looked away and then up at the stars. When he looked back he saw she was still staring at him. Those eyes.

'Are you happy, Philip?' she asked. He laughed. 'I mean really happy?'

'Yes, I'm content. I think I'm pretty lucky, really.'

But she persisted: 'That's not what I asked. Are you happy?'

'Blimey, Jane. I don't know. Do you mean if I could would I change anything? I'd like to be younger, and a bit richer maybe. And slimmer. But as I say, I think I've been very lucky.'

'Any regrets?'

'I wish I hadn't given up learning to play the piano after only two lessons.'

'No, seriously.'

He looked at her, trying to work out what she was getting at. And then he said it. 'I wish the summer of 1977 had lasted for ever.' He felt his heart start to beat more quickly.

She looked at him. He was desperate for her to say the same thing, but he knew she wouldn't. She looked at her wine glass and then at her watch. He noticed the little moles on her arm. She then shocked him by putting her hand on his and asked if he would walk her to the station. He stared at her hand. He remembered driving her car. The hedgehog's guts.

'Of course. I'd love to. You'd better drink up, too; we ought to go.'

They set off, Jane again putting her arm through his. He considered taking her hand but decided he was better off settling for arm in arm rather than risking taking her hand only for it to be withdrawn. The High Street was surprisingly quiet. They saw three girls in tight short skirts staggering down a side street, giggling hysterically. A bearded young man, homeless and hungry according to the dirty piece of card propped up by his feet, looked up as they passed, asking them silently to add to the meagre contents of his upturned cap. Philip found himself humming the slow movement of Rachmaninov's Piano Concerto No. 2, and then apologised for doing so. He knew some people found it irritating, even rude, when others hummed or whistled for no apparent reason.

'What about you?' he asked.

'What *about* me?'

'Are *you* happy?'

'Oh, I don't know. I've been happy today. I'm very happy we bumped into each other. They were good times, weren't they?' She dipped into her bag and brought out her phone. 'Can you let me have your mobile number, and you take mine. Let me know when you next come to London. Come soon.'

They had arrived outside the station and quickly added each other's details to their contacts lists. Philip remembered the airport farewell forty years earlier and suddenly his mouth felt dry. He couldn't wait another forty years.

'Bye, Jane. It's been the best Saturday I've had for years.'

'Foregate Street. Not Milford Junction.'

He looked at her, asking for an explanation, but she simply smiled. He hugged her and then moved to kiss her on the cheek. But she turned her head and he was kissing her on the lips. He felt an instantaneous shock of electricity and immediately recalled the taste of her lips when they had shared their first kiss. She was holding him tight. It was Philip who broke away this time, immediately regretting doing so but not having the courage to return for more. *How long would she have let that last?* he thought.

'Bye, Philip. Come to London. Soon. Come tomorrow.'

She turned and walked through the doors into the station and didn't turn back. *What was she thinking now?* he wondered. That kiss. And she had squeezed him tightly. Like on the Ponte Vecchio. He had felt the shape of her breasts against his chest. He had smelt her. Not just her perfume, not Charlie now, but her. The smell of her hair, her skin, her sixty years of being Jane. Still beautiful Jane. He had tasted her lips, the sweetness of her lip-gloss and the gentle sourness of the white wine she had drunk. He wondered what she had tasted of him. He held his hand up in front of his mouth and breathed out, relieved that he couldn't detect anything unpleasant. He thought he would run into the station and rush to her platform, but he let good sense stop him, and he turned to walk back to where his car was parked on the Green, feeling confused and frustrated, but also elated and more alive than he had felt for years. He whistled the Rachmaninov again, and remembered the scene towards the end of *Brief Encounter* when Dolly Messiter arrives in the station waiting room to ruin the last few moments Alec and Laura have together and David Lean, the director, uses an extreme close-up of her gabbling mouth. Of course: Milford Junction! But Dolly's mouth became confused with Jane's in his mind and he was savouring their kiss again, hardly able to believe it had happened. He found the Rachmaninov in the music library on his phone and played it through Bluetooth in the car. The taste of her mouth and her breasts pushing against his ribs were all he could think of as he drove home.

Laura said she couldn't wait any longer and had eaten some cheese and biscuits and opened a bottle of Rioja. He said he'd enjoyed the concert and had enjoyed chatting with his old friend Jane. He poured himself a glass and Laura refused his offer of a top-up. She was watching a recording of an episode of *Lewis*. They'd seen it before, Philip quickly realised, and both knew exactly how it ended, but he happily sat down to watch with her. There was something comforting about the unhurried rhythms of either a *Lewis* or an *Endeavour*, though neither was a patch on *Morse*. More often than not, Philip's attention would wander during an episode and it quickly did so now. He pictured Jane on the train and was tempted to text her but felt that he shouldn't while Laura was in the room and anyway, he was worried it would seem a bit desperate. *Shall I or shan't I?* She had made him feel that she would welcome his attentions. It was her idea to get each other's mobile numbers. But he couldn't be sure. Was he imagining feelings on her part that were only really the simple pleasure of seeing again an old friend? He should wait for her to make contact again. That would be best. Less chance of embarrassment or humiliation. Less chance of any advances being rejected.

But she had kissed him on the mouth.

10

APRIL 1977

FLORENCE

Their two days in Florence were to include a full morning in the Uffizi, an afternoon at The Accademia and the next morning at the Medici Chapel. They were staying in a simple but convenient hotel near Santa Maria Novella, in three single rooms.

Washed and changed, they strolled along the Via Panzani in search of somewhere to eat and found a small trattoria that was nearly full of locals – a good sign, they all agreed. The Fiorentini all seemed to be talking at the same time, drinking their wine and wiping their bread to get the last burst of flavour from their pasta sauces, gesticulating extravagantly, smoking.

David told Jane and Philip something about the plans he had for the summer's outdoor production of *Macbeth*, and they were both surprised when he indicated he wanted to stage the play in modern dress because his productions were usually very traditional, and he had always hired Elizabethan or Jacobean costumes from Stratford for the Shakespeare plays he had produced. Philip liked the modern dress idea very much. He said he had read an essay about the play called, 'How many children had Lady Macbeth?' by L C Knights and said it had made him think about the whole business of children in the play and why the Witches didn't prophesy that Macbeth's children would become kings. Their discussion arrived at the view that one way of playing the relationship was to imagine the Macbeths had lost a child and not been able to have any more. 'Yes,' Jane said, staring at Philip, tempting him to visualise, he thought. 'She says, "*I have given suck and know how tender 'tis to love the babe that milks me.*"' All three agreed the theory gave a particular resonance to a number of other lines in the play and could help to explain the relationship between husband and wife and her methods of persuasion. Suddenly, Philip remembered the photograph on the bookcase in David's dining room and glanced at Jane in panic, but then he saw to his great relief that David didn't seem discomposed but was happily eating away, demonstrating complete mastery with his spaghetti fork.

David sought their approval for the other casting ideas he had in mind, and neither Jane nor Philip was surprised by them, chiefly because both were so excited about the prospect of playing opposite each other that even the weirdest notions would have gone unchallenged.

Jane had enjoyed her bruschetta and linguini al granchio, and Philip and David their spaghetti alla puttanesca and bistecca alla Fiorentina, and they had shared a bottle of Chianti Classico. Having paid, David said it was time for him to retire for the night, thanked them for their company, said he would meet them for breakfast in the hotel at 8.30 the following morning, and then got up and left. Both Jane and Philip were aware that his departure was his way of leaving the two of them alone together, and Philip was pleased that Jane seemed as happy about this as he was.

'He that's going must be provided for,' Jane said, when David had left the restaurant, and Philip smiled, but then said, 'What's that supposed to mean?'

'It would just be nice if we had more time to ourselves. Maybe we should get up early in the morning and drive to Rome in his car and leave him behind.'

'That would be quite funny, wouldn't it? A bit on the mean side, perhaps. What is it about you and cars!'

'Where's your spirit of adventure? Have you lost it, then?'

'It still exists, I promise. He's been very good to me, you know. I wouldn't be at university if he hadn't told me I should apply. I wouldn't have been involved in *Twelfth Night*.'

Philip suggested they have a Strega for a nightcap, but Jane declined so they got up and left the restaurant. They walked side by side, close, and Philip sensed he could take Jane's hand and she wouldn't resist. It felt cool, smooth and small, and he hoped his wasn't too hot and clammy. He wanted to hold it forever.

'Why don't we walk across to the Boboli gardens?' he suggested, determined to prolong his evening with her.

'I'm too tired for that, Philip. It's a lovely idea, I know, but it's also getting a little chilly.' He feared she was anxious to get back to the hotel and felt a sense of deflation, but then she took her hand from his and wrapped her arm around his waist. Instantaneously cheered, he put his arm around her shoulder and was surprised again at how slight she was.

He watched the two of them strolling towards the Campanile, a perfect fit, all movements cohering, the girl beautiful beyond measure, the boy completely devoted. *Patience rewarded*, he thought.

She leant her head on his chest and then stopped walking to tell him that she could hear his heart beating.

'I remember when I first saw you,' Philip said. 'It was on the mail boat, over a year ago. I was going to Guernsey with the school to play football. You were with your sister, Jenny, I think. I swear I have thought about you nearly every day since then. I couldn't believe it when you appeared at the first *Twelfth Night* rehearsal. Those rehearsals were the highlight of my week and I couldn't wait from one to the next. I was worried you didn't like me. I was so jealous when you were friendly with Tony. Did you know what I was thinking during that time?'

'I remember being on the boat. We were going to Guernsey to play in a concert, I think, but I don't remember seeing you.'

'You were wearing a gold and purple midi skirt and a baggy cream over-sized pullover.'

'How can you remember that?' She smiled at him. 'During rehearsals I wasn't even sure you liked me; I sometimes thought you were picking on me. It was different when we did *Streetcar*.' She looked down at her feet and then back up at him. Her eyes. He had never looked so intently at anyone or anything. *Two of the fairest stars.* They promised unfathomable joys. 'I'm sorry I upset you,' she continued. 'I didn't want to get hurt and I didn't want to hurt you. There was hardly any of the summer left, Philip.' He loved it when she spoke his name; it was confirmation she really was speaking to him. Philip Robinson. 'But we've got all of this summer to look forward to, haven't we?' She stopped, turned to face him fully, put her arms around his waist and her cheek on his chest, and held him tight. He smelt her hair, its citrus fragrance. When she released him he looked at her and tentatively leant forward to kiss her, and she did not move away. *Yes. Yes. Yes.* Those lips. It was happening. She slowly stopped the kiss and looked at him, her face very serious. She moved towards him and they kissed again, and the world stopped turning. The sweetest taste. The softest touch. He had only ever kissed three girls before in real life. On the first occasion, at a drunken fancy dress party, he had been shocked at the ferocity of the girl and his main priority had been to avoid injury. The second girl had been gentle and kind, but her breath had never tasted sweet or fresh and she had been even more tentative than him. And the girl he'd met at a party at university had tried to swallow his face. Jane's lips, the evolutionary perfection he had imagined kissing so often, were smooth and moist. She flicked the tip of her tongue across the inside of his lips, catching his tongue, and for a moment he felt unable to breathe so delicious was the shock. This was the best moment of his life. Here he was, in one of the world's great cities, alone with a girl whom he had worshipped, mostly from afar, for a year and a half, who had the most beautiful face he had ever seen and she was kissing him in a way which made his whole body ache with pleasure and longing, with fire and ice. For a beautiful moment he thought he might cry, but then she lifted her hands to cradle his face. He wanted the moment to last forever. She moved her hands to his hips. He thought someone had dropped ice cubes down the back of his shirt and was relieved when she moved back, because he was struggling to deal with his own pleasure.

"'*You kiss by the book,*'" she said. "'*Give me my kiss again.*'" He smiled in recognition. He took her face in his hands, and she moved her hands from his hips and placed them on his buttocks. They kissed again, Philip's tongue tentatively seeking hers, and when she pressed her pelvis against his, he instinctively moved his hands from her face in a moment of panic, but he immediately realised he could no longer conceal the nature or extent of his pleasure. '*If it were now to die, 'twere now to be most happy,'* he thought. She broke away and looked up at him, and he felt her eyes almost overwhelming him with erotic promises.

'I love you. I have loved you from the moment I first saw you,' he said. But not out loud.

11

AUGUST 2018

SATURDAY
WORCESTER

'Come to London. Soon. Come Tomorrow.' Her very words, and they had been said with some urgency. 'Tomorrow'! It hadn't just been a casual invitation, made in the certain knowledge that it would not be taken up.

Philip was sitting in his study upstairs. Laura was still downstairs, still watching *Lewis*. He was on his laptop exploring all-inclusive holidays for the following Easter in countries offering some early summer warmth. He was also investigating city breaks in Florence and Rome and thinking of Jane.

'Come to London. Soon. Come Tomorrow,' she had said. Philip hadn't been able to dismiss the words. *How can she have so much power over me, after all this time?* he thought. He had found himself playing the words over and over in his head. He could easily hop on a train at any time or drive down, but he needed to have a reason to give to Laura for making such a trip. He remembered that Jane's husband would be away until Wednesday and felt desperate to find a way to justify a trip tomorrow or the day after.

He could hear the television immediately below him in the sitting room and knew Laura would still be engrossed. But he wanted to make sure. He went downstairs and asked Laura if she wanted her wine topped up. 'Yes, please,' she said without her eyes leaving the screen. He went to the kitchen, picked up the bottle of Rioja and carried it through. He half-filled her glass and she thanked him, looking away from the screen for a couple of seconds and smiling. He returned the bottle to the kitchen, topped himself up more generously and went back upstairs. He sat again at his desk, took a large gulp of wine and picked up his phone.

I could come to London tomorrow but need a pretext, he typed. He stared at the words on the screen. He was trying to anticipate the possible consequences of sending the text, balancing the equation of risk and reward. He couldn't resist the prospect of seeing her again and being alone with her. He pressed send. Straight after he thought that he shouldn't have referred to a pretext because it implied guilt and also hope, both of which were obviously premature. But she *had* said, 'Come to London. Soon. Come tomorrow.'

He thought there might be an immediate reply. He hoped there would be, even if it was just to acknowledge receipt of his text, and he stared at his screen, willing a reply to pop up. He remembered counting to a hundred. But there was nothing.

Still nothing.

Still nothing.

He started to feel sick with anxiety. What had he done? It was stupid to have sent the text. What did he think it could possibly achieve?

And then there was a ping and his eyes flew to the screen. But it was John from his tennis WhatsApp group asking who was going to play on Wednesday evening. Philip knew that this would mean a series of replies from the dozen or so members of the group. Sure enough, three responses came straight away. Philip thought about what could conceivably happen before his mates met to play on Wednesday. Would he be going to London? Would he still be there? Would he ever play tennis with them again? He made himself slow down, and accepted that in all probability this week would actually be no different from other weeks. Two more WhatsApp replies. Back to the real world; his prosaic world.

He looked around his study and his eyes fell upon a row of art books, amongst them some guides to galleries, including one about the Uffizi. He pulled out this volume, opened it at a random page and found himself in the Botticelli room, looking at prints of *Primavera* and *The Birth of Venus*.

12

APRIL 1977

FLORENCE

Philip and Jane had walked to the Piazza della Signoria, hoping it would be quieter than during the day, but there was a young performer juggling and eating fire who had attracted a large crowd. He looked at Jane and saw the flames reflected in one of her eyes, illuminating one side of her face, turning her olive complexion a golden orange. They had watched the entertainment for a short while before deciding to make their way back to the hotel. Jane had said that when they visited the Uffizi tomorrow they needed to make sure they didn't get stuck with David. She suggested they propose to him that they all do their own thing and agree to meet at a specific time at a specific place. Philip thought David would be well aware what Jane was contriving but would be perfectly happy to acquiesce to her request.

They had both been surprised at how late it was when they reached the hotel. They collected their room keys from reception and headed up the narrow staircase to the first floor.

Philip was happy that Jane was ahead of him because she would arrive at her door before him and would have to decide how the evening was to end. She had managed the situation with complete assurance, unlocking her door, turning to Philip and saying, 'That was a lovely evening. Thank you. See you tomorrow,' before kissing him briefly, turning away and walking into her room, closing the door behind her. He had stood outside her room, staring at the door and trying to imagine what she was doing. He wanted to believe she was standing on the other side, leaning on the door, eyes closed in longing, wishing she'd invited him in. He wanted to knock on the door to force her to come out just so that he could say, 'I love you,' but he knew that just for once he should try to be sensible and patient and simply enjoy the fact that he had had an amazing evening and they had kissed for the first time.

At breakfast the following morning, David was very lively and keen to ask Jane about the course she had just been on. Philip was happy to let the two of them converse. He reflected on how little sleep he had had whereas Jane looked perfect, eyes bright and complexion silken. He marvelled at her elegant posture: she was sitting well forward on her chair, back straight, beautiful neck effortlessly supporting a sculpted head polished to perfection. She was wearing a pale blue linen dress with narrow straps exposing her shoulders and collarbone. Her skin was totally without blemish and he looked at it and imagined stroking and kissing it. As she leant forward for the milk jug, he caught a glimpse of her armpit and a bra strap and some more flesh. He remembered the pinafore dress and the freshly shaved armpit at David's dinner party. He thought there would be no painting or sculpture later that morning in the Uffizi to compare with her beauty.

He looked at David. He had dropped crumbs from his bread roll down the front of his shirt where there was a fresh coffee stain, hardly surprising given the enthusiasm with which he was trying to combine breakfast and conversation.

Philip caught Jane's eye. He didn't say anything but simply tried to read her mind. Had yesterday evening meant the same for her as it had for him? He thought about how she had pressed against him. What had she thought? Suddenly he realised David was talking to him.

'Sorry, David. I was miles away.'

'I was asking if there were things you particularly wanted to see in the Uffizi this morning.'

'I don't really know what's there, apart from the Botticellis.'

'I think you should look at the fourteenth-century work before you move on to the early renaissance rooms. What about you, Jane?'

'I spent some time looking at the earlier work last week on my course, so I'd like to concentrate on the next rooms, rooms 10–14 especially.' She looked hard at Philip. 'The Botticellis are in one of those, I think.' She continued to look at him, clearly expecting him to take some initiative to ensure they would not have to spend the whole morning with David.

'We can speak further about this when we get there,' Philip said, before topping up David's coffee and his own in an attempt to put a lid on the subject.

After a brief return to their rooms, they re-gathered outside the hotel and made their way towards the Uffizi, David leading the way. The streets were busy, and walking on the sunny side meant they could already feel some spring warmth. David insisted on stopping regularly to point out a piece of architecture or some religious iconography, while Jane was just as happy to look at shop windows and Philip was happy to look at her.

The Piazza della Signoria looked glorious in the morning sunshine, and an already quite lengthy queue outside the

Uffizi didn't seem to mind waiting while in such beautiful surroundings. Dozens of people surrounded the statue of *David*, many of them more concerned to get some good photographs than they were actually to look at it. Philip heard a guide explain, to the audible surprise of his party, that this was only a replica of the original statue in the Accademia.

There seemed to be so many Americans and very few Italians. There were a lot of young rucksacked couples, and Philip envied them their confidence in each other that allowed them to show their mutual affections so naturally. He noticed the casual ease with which they held and touched each other in ways that to him seemed really quite intimate. Jane caught his wandering eye and asked him simply with her facial expression how they were going to manage 'losing' David while in the gallery.

The queue moved gratifyingly quickly and they were soon inside. Philip surprised himself by announcing, 'Right, it's 10.05. I think we should do our own things and meet up at 11.30 in the rooftop bar for coffee, and then maybe we can decide to go and look at something together.' Jane agreed, rather too quickly, he thought, but David smiled and did not seem inclined to spoil their plan even if he would almost certainly have preferred to have their company. Jane headed off in one direction and Philip deliberately set off in another direction in what he knew was a completely futile attempt to fool David about their intentions.

A minute later, Philip was wondering where on earth he was and which direction he should go in, envisaging the worst – that she'd given up waiting for him and disappeared. When he finally joined her, some minutes later, he tried to recover from a mild panic, protested he'd lost his bearings and suggested the gallery map was pretty useless. Jane simply smiled. Then she took his hand and led him to *The Birth of Venus*. Standing in front of one of the best-known images of the world's artistic heritage, Philip was imagining Jane standing on the scallop shell and involuntarily he squeezed her hand a little tighter. She looked at him and Philip thought she was reading his mind.

'Do you think she's beautiful?' she asked. 'Apparently, neo-platonic philosophers believed that contemplating her beauty was a way to elevate the human spirit and get closer to the divine.'

'She doesn't elevate my spirit, or anything else for that matter.' Philip couldn't quite believe what he had just said. Nevertheless, he looked at Jane and it was clear to him she was also thinking about last night.

'Probably just as well: not really the time and the place,' she said.

They held hands as they walked through other rooms, not saying much and not staying long at any of the paintings until they found themselves alone in the Dosso Dossi room in front of a work called *Witchcraft*.

'What an extraordinary image,' Philip offered. 'Look at their faces. What on earth is she doing?'

Jane said, '"*Come to my woman's breasts*"...'

'You said a few minutes ago it wasn't the time or the place.'

'"*And take my milk for gall, you murdering ministers.*"'

'What lovely apples.'

Jane seemed to be lost in the moment, and when Philip looked at her his humour disappeared and he felt he might be caught in her thrall. But then she suddenly smiled, and they both enjoyed his innuendo.

'I can't wait for the summer and for rehearsals to start,' Jane said. 'I'm going to have you just here,' she added, pointing to the palm of her outstretched hand.

'Promises, promises!' Again Philip had surprised himself. 'But, in the meantime, we'd better go and meet David in the café. Tell you what, you can lead the way.'

13

AUGUST 2018

SATURDAY
WORCESTER

He was staring at Venus, her hair reminding him of Cosette's hair on posters for the musical of *Les Misérables*, though the zephyr was blowing it in the opposite direction. He started to sing Eponine's song, 'On My Own', reflecting on how her predicament was similar to Viola's in *Twelfth Night*, and he was taken back to the school production all that time ago when he had worked with Jane for the first time. '*Most radiant, exquisite and unmatchable beauty.*' He had thought that then and still thought it now. 'All good wishes' – and he remembered tossing the card onto his bedroom floor.

He returned to looking at holidays in the Canaries and Cape Verde, anywhere he and Laura could go next half-term holiday to stretch out the late summer or early autumn with more sunshine and warmth. He thought how nice it would be if the boys could join them, knowing full well it wouldn't happen. They hadn't holidayed as a family for years: the boys had their own lives and went to much more exotic locations than he and Laura could afford.

Ping. His heart lurched. But it was one of the WhatsApp tennis players saying, 'Not me this week.' He thought he'd better let everyone know his plans, too, and was typing, '*Me neither,*' when another text appeared, from Jane. His heart leapt again. He quickly sent the tennis WhatsApp and fumbled to bring up Jane's text.

'*The pretext is up to you. But come to London. Soon. Come tomorrow. X*'

He noticed the kiss and inhaled sharply. He saw her lips. He tasted them. *It isn't as easy as that, Jane,* he thought. Another tennis WhatsApp pinged in, and he saw the one he had sent a minute earlier. He'd typed, '*Mr neither,*' and felt embarrassed and cross with himself. He hated that kind of carelessness even though he knew it was fantastically unimportant. He remembered a brief, informal email correspondence he had once had with a distinguished academic about one of his former students. Philip had been surprised that the prof in his emails had made all sorts of typos, sometimes using lower case when it should have been upper case, and paragraphing randomly. It didn't actually matter, did it? Communication was still perfectly clear. He wasn't illiterate. He was brilliant! And busy. So he told himself not to worry about his typo and that only a sad neurotic would bother to send a correction.

He decided to google what was on in London but found nothing useful. He could hear from downstairs what he knew was the music at the end of *Lewis* and he decided to go down.

'Has it finished? Shall we just watch the news?' Yes to both.

When the news had finished, Laura said, 'Come on, let's have a stroll up the garden?'

It was so still and there were millions of stars in the sky. They sat on the chairs on the round patio and Laura observed how peaceful and quiet it was.

Then they both saw a bat swoop and climb and head towards the house. Laura said, 'Do you remember that time when we had a bat in our bedroom?'

'Yes, and I remember extremely clearly how you said you couldn't possibly sleep and demanded I should do something to get it out.'

'You wouldn't have slept either,' she insisted.

'I would, and I was perfectly happy to read until it found its own way out. It's the same with moths.'

'How can you read when a moth is flapping against your lampshade?'

'I can't but I know it will disappear at some point. "I'm looking for the Pleiades, the Seven Sisters, but these girls are not out tonight. Oh, yes they are, there they are."'

'Where?'

'No idea. I don't know what they look like. "How pretty the sky is! I ought to go there on a rocket that never comes down."'

Laura recognised the quotations; she'd heard them before, more than once. But she was not in the mood for Tennessee Williams and changed the subject. 'Rosemary and Jack invited us to supper on Tuesday, but I said it was our turn to host so they're coming to us. That's OK, isn't it?'

'That's great, yes. It will be nice to see them.'

'I was constructing the menu while doing aqua aerobics. I'd like to do something really healthy, so how about my harissa salmon dish with pak choi and mushrooms? I don't think we should bother with a starter, and I'll do a lemon syllabub for pudding. And we can have some cheese if you want.'

'They both like their cheese, don't they?'

'Yes, I know. You can do the shopping on Tuesday while I'm at work, can't you?'

'I should be able to fit that in, yes. Although I do have a newspaper to read and the garden really is begging to have someone sit in it.'

'You wait until the week after next when I'm on holiday. I shall expect to be waited on. I'm looking forward to lots of cycle rides and some long walks.'

'You never allow me to wait on you. You're rubbish at doing nothing.'

'Just as well, really, given how good you are at it. Must be all the practice you've had over the years.'

'It's important to make best use of the talents you've been given.'

'Don't start getting all biblical with me!' They sat in amiable contentment for a short while, looking at the stars. They both started to realise that the peaceful stillness they were enjoying wasn't completely silent: the air was filled with unidentified little whispers and ticks and wheezes and clicks. 'Just think,' she said. 'This time next year, you'll be retired. What are we going to do to mark your retirement? Where would you like to go?'

'Pizza Express?'

'No, come on. Seriously?'

'The Mercedes garage?'

'Be serious, Philip. This is important. It's going to be a very special moment. Thirty-five years. What about New Zealand? I'd love to go there. The scenery is incredible. I was chatting to a new girl at work a few days ago. She's only just started with us, just graduated, and she was telling me about her time there in her gap year. She went to cliffs and fjords and geysers. To volcanoes and the Southern Alps. Apparently the south island is brilliant for wildlife. She says she saw whales and penguins. And albatrosses.'

'Hope she didn't shoot any of them.'

'Don't be ridiculous. What are you talking about? Would you fancy that? I think I could probably get quite a lot of time off work so we could go for a month, maybe longer.' She was getting excited at the prospect. Her enthusiasm and imagination were fired, and he loved the way she was talking more quickly and starting to forget to breathe in her excitement. 'Let's do it. You'll have a nice lump sum and you can't just stick it all in a savings account. Carpe diem and all that.'

'Yes, carpe diem. I completely agree with that. But would you really like to spend twenty-four hours on a plane?'

'No, I wouldn't look forward to that bit. But on those flights you eat and sleep and read and watch films. You're very good at all of those. Especially the eating. And the sleeping, actually.'

'I sleep well because I have a clear conscience, that's why.'

'Yes, that must be it.' After a brief silence, she asked, 'Come on, where would you most like to go?'

He sought inspiration in the stars. 'I can see the attraction of New Zealand for sure. It's an exciting thought. But we should also go to Italy again, sometime, don't you think? Florence and Rome.'

'Mmm, yes, I'd love to.' She sighed contentedly. 'Well, we'll have plenty of time to go to all sorts of places, won't we? Especially after I've retired as well. And that's only two years away.' They looked at each other and she smiled. He smiled back. A preoccupied smile.

She stood up and looked down at him and said, 'I think the dew is coming down. Let's go in,' and she offered him a hand which he took and she pulled him out of his chair. 'Come on, old man. It's past your bedtime.'

'I'll come in in a minute. I'm going to have a final little potter, if I can manage it without my walking stick.'

He watched her walk towards the house and knew that he shouldn't go to London. How could he want more than what he had? He loved what he had. It was forty years ago. It was a ridiculous idea. He looked at his phone. There were no more messages – from Jane or his tennis mates. He clicked on the last message from Jane and saw the cursor blinking in the text box ready for him to type.

But he didn't know what to say. He clicked off the app and walked down the garden towards the house, enjoying the scent of lavender heavy in the air. Carpe diem, she'd said. Carpe diem.

14

LATE JULY 1977

JERSEY

It was a balmy evening at Myrtle Manor, the beautiful location for their outdoor production of *Macbeth*. The lawns had been mown earlier in the day and the smell of newly cut grass and the night-scented stock and jasmine was intense and intoxicating. With still over six weeks to go until opening night, David had been rehearsing with Jane and Philip alone, the rest of the cast being given a Friday off. They were running all of the scenes they had together while David watched, reading in lines when necessary, hunched up in his chair, hands wrapped round a flask of black coffee, in Zhivago fur hat, worn for the image, not the unnecessary insulation it was providing. He didn't interrupt but simply enjoyed the fact that they had already arrived at the point when he was confident it was going to be a great show. They had started the rehearsal period a month earlier with Philip saying that Harold Bloom had said the Macbeths' marriage was the best in Shakespeare and they had pursued this idea and allowed it to inform all of their scenes.

"'Come, we'll to sleep. My strange and self-abuse
Is the initiate fear that wants hard use.
We are yet but young indeed.'"

'Very good, you two!' David said. 'Well done. *"To bed, to bed, to bed."* Time to go home. If you're as good as that when we have the full run on Sunday the rest of the cast will realise they have to raise their game.'

'Thanks, David. Yes, that felt good. What a play! I love it,' Philip said.

'I'd like to have another go at act 1 scene 7. I spoilt it because I muddled up a couple of the lines,' Jane said.

David protested, 'Did you? So what, Jane? It's amazing you both know them already. I'm afraid you'll have to do it without your director, if you don't mind. And I'm sure you don't, Jane. I'm going home.'

Jane's reply was delivered immediately and with a smile. David was not remotely put out, ostentatiously cleared his throat, smiled back and shuffled off towards his car, his chair folded down and tucked under his arm, vacuum flask in one hand and script in the other. They watched him reach his car, put the chair in the boot, get behind the wheel, start up and kangaroo jump away, spitting up the gravel as he went.

Philip turned to Jane and she slowly walked ahead, clearly expecting him to follow. He was on an invisible lead.

'Do you really want to have another go at that scene?' Philip asked.

'Yes, but just the words. Let's do it sitting down. Over here.' She delved into her enormous straw bag and pulled out the picnic blanket she always brought to rehearsal. She spread it out next to the huge rhododendron bush that served as the wings stage right. She sat down and Philip sat next to her, at which point she stretched out, lay down on her back and closed her eyes. He thought he could happily look at her forever, and never feel the need to see another living soul. He looked at her eyelids, gossamer smooth. He saw her nose and the most perfect small round nostrils. And her lips. He believed he would never love anything more or see anything so beautiful. He thought she must know he was looking at her and he remembered what she had said three months ago in the Uffizi: 'I'm going to have you just here,' indicating the palm of her hand. She was right. At that moment he knew he would do anything she asked him to do, if refusing to do so meant he would never see her again.

'Are we going to do the scene, then?' she asked, but leaving him no choice.

He lay down alongside her, close enough to hear her breathing, close enough to sense her chest rising and falling. He closed his eyes and began.

> *"I have no spur*
> *To prick the sides of my intent but only*
> *Vaulting ambition which o'erleaps itself*
> *And falls on the other.*
> *How now? What news?"'*
> *"'He has almost supped. Why have you left the chamber?"'*
> *"'Hath he asked for me?"'*
> *"'Know you not he has?"'*
> *"'We will proceed no further in this business.*
> *He hath honoured me of late, and I have bought*
> *Golden opinions from all sorts of people*
> *Which would be worn no in their newest gloss,*
> *Not cast aside so soon."'*
> *"'Was the hope drunk*
> *Wherein you drest yourself?"'*

Philip, eyes closed still, felt her move and knew that she was sitting up and leaning over him, staring accusingly.

> *"'Hath it slept since?*

And wakes it now to look so green and pale
At what it did so freely? From this time
Such I account thy love. Art thou afeard
To be the same in thine own act and valour
As thou art in desire? Wouldst thou have that
Which thou esteem'st the ornament of life,
And live a coward in thine own esteem,
Letting "I dare not" wait upon "I would",
Like the poor cat i'the adage."
Philip opened his eyes and sat up and stared back.
"'Prithee peace.
I dare do all that may become a man;
Who dares do more is none.'"
She pretended to start to cry.
"'What beast was't then
That made you break this enterprise to me?
When you durst do it then you were a man;'"
She leant a hand on his shoulder and he gave in to the
pressure and lay down again. She slipped her hand onto his
thigh and whispered into his ear:
"'And to be more than what you were, you would
Be so much more the man."'
She stretched out all of the words as her hand slipped
under his T-shirt and sweater and gently stroked his stomach.
She moved it higher to his chest. Philip didn't move. He
stopped breathing and kept his eyes closed, afraid that if he
opened them the moment would be lost and he would discover
he was imagining it all. Her hand moved down and when
it reached his abdomen his own hand stopped it. His hand
rested on hers and he held his breath again. He could hear
and feel her steady breathing. Slowly she moved her fingers,
stroking his belly. He gently lifted his hand and lifted both
arms above his head, breathing through his mouth in short

staccato snatches. Her fingers edged beneath the belt line of his jeans and briefly brushed the tip of his penis through his underpants. He pointed his toes, tightening his calves, and clenched his buttocks. She slowly sat up and undid the button at the top of his jeans and gently lowered the zip, with the other hand resting protectively on his underpants. He raised his buttocks to help her lower his jeans. She leant forward and rested her head on his stomach, stroking the top of his inside thigh. He was too scared to move. Then she lifted her head and he didn't know what would follow until he felt her lips on his and her tongue gently seeking a way into his mouth. And then her fingers again were on his belly, finding a way into his pants. Briefly the world stopped and he knew he would soon die. He tried to think of something else, but she had taken him in her hand and was slowly squeezing and stroking, squeezing and stretching, her tongue gently exploring his mouth. He had never felt like this before. Never. Never. He couldn't last any longer. He stopped her hand with his own and she sat up as he held his breath, and nearly two years of desperate longing was suddenly released.

15

AUGUST 2018

SATURDAY
PARIS

Bill King was sitting on a stool, legs spread, in the bar of the Lancaster Hotel in the Rue de Berri in Paris, just off the Champs-Élysées. It was a stiflingly hot early evening and the doors from the bar into the adjacent courtyard were closed and the air-conditioning was working hard. The baccarat crystal chandelier and Louis XV and XVI period furniture afforded the room a feeling of unashamed luxury and sophistication. A grey and cream palette provided the counterpoint, suggesting an intimacy and discretion. *Yes, life is good*, Bill thought.

He was sipping his glass of Chassagne Montrachet, savouring the combination of fruit and mineral, surprised but not displeased by how oaky it was. He was feeling relaxed, freshly showered, and wearing a comfortable and immaculate Charles Tyrrwhit shirt, happy that earlier in the afternoon business had been completed on one of the deals he was in Paris to negotiate.

He took his phone out of his trouser pocket, saw he had two texts from Jane, glanced at them but did not reply. She knew he was going to be busy. He had a quick flick through his Twitter feed, and then placed the phone on the bar, having made sure that it was on silent. He took another sip of wine and swirled it around in his mouth, before swallowing and slowly nodding, lips pursed as if about to kiss someone. A strikingly tall woman, in her thirties, he estimated, appeared at the other end of the bar, dressed in a grey suit and looking exotically stylish. He wondered how she could appear so cool dressed as she was and in this heat. He stared at her, hoping to attract her eye, and he looked at her long, shapely legs, but she studiously ignored him until her drink was served and she turned from the bar to go to her seat at a corner table, looking at him briefly with an expression that even the supremely complacent Bill could not confuse for anything other than disdain. He sipped his wine again, catching the barman's eye to ask for replenishment. The barman himself shared the lady's contempt for his customer but complied with his request with perfect professionalism.

Bill looked at his watch. She was late. Only ten minutes, but enough to make him feel irritated. He picked up his phone again and swiped through some photos before checking the balance of some accounts using his banking app. He had known for three or four years that he no longer needed to work, but the alternative held few attractions. He looked forward to the week more than the weekend. There was still a buzz about working on a deal, and he enjoyed meeting all kinds of people, many of them highly intelligent and driven, some stupid, some corrupt and some wealthy on an almost unimaginable scale. And some of them were young, exciting, dangerous and did amazing things to his ego.

A striking forty-year-old woman arrived at his side. In Bill's mind she looked astonishingly like Juliette Binoche.

She was wearing her hair up in a bun and large shades. Her brilliant white silk blouse was only partially tucked into her black trousers at one side hanging loosely over her hip; studiously casual. Around her neck she wore a gold medallion necklace, a dozen or so small diamonds contained within a convex glass circle set inside the gold frame. Her black shoes had four-inch heels, a thin strap over her toes and a wider one across the top of her ankle, on which were small gold rings looking like coins, a design also reflected in the edging of her black leather bag.

'Bill,' she said, offering him one cheek and then the other. 'I hope you did not think I was not coming. Julian was very chatty in the office and it was not easy to leave. There was hardly anything to do all day until it is very nearly time to leave.'

'Well, you're here now, so sit down and have a drink.' The barman was already pouring her a glass of wine, his face working hard to hide his thought that she was wasted on this man sitting smugly alongside her.

'Ah, a Montrachet; *un bon choix*,' she said as she took a large gulp, then breathed in and out slowly and deeply before looking up at him and smiling.

They had met during one of Bill's previous visits to Paris on business. She was PA to a senior associate at a law firm with which Bill's firm did a lot of work, and had been present at an evening dinner to celebrate the completion of a deal. Bill had found himself sitting next to her, discovered very early on that she was a recent divorcee and was pleased when she seemed as happy to flirt with him as he was to flirt with her and equally keen to exchange phone numbers. On the three further occasions since that trip when Bill had been in Paris they had met up for drinks, dinner and sex, not always in that order.

She had endured for ten years a marriage that had become loveless and had been enjoying for the last two years the freedom to come and go as she pleased. She did not enquire too much into his private life. But he had told her she was the lucky one. His marriage was also loveless, but they still shared the same house. His wife was no longer able to be the focus of attention she had always been, no longer had the power to distract all red-blooded men, but had become a bitter and deeply unhappy woman, someone he had stopped loving many years ago. He had told her he did not think she could do any further harm to a marriage that was irretrievably broken, and clearly neither felt any compunction about committing adultery.

'Would you like to eat here or elsewhere?' he asked.

'Oh, let's stay 'ere. We know it is very good, and we will not 'ave to walk very far, will we? Just a few steps to climb to our usual room, I assume? I can just about manage that.'

He smiled, and then rudely gestured to the barman to instruct him to pour them both more wine and then to open another bottle. He would not be enjoying evenings like this if he were retired and spent all his time at home.

16

AUGUST 2018

SUNDAY
WORCESTER TO LONDON

As they were drinking their cafetière of coffee in bed the following morning, Laura reminded Philip she had arranged to go for a walk with Angela after church and then was going to visit her mother in the care home in Malvern and would maybe take her out for tea if she felt up to it.

'Come with us, if you like,' she added, but he knew she expected him to say no. Her mother didn't recognise him anymore, and Laura knew that he found it difficult. She was also perfectly aware there was Premiership football for him to watch.

'I'd prefer to stay here to work in the garden, to be honest. You don't mind, do you?'

'Of course not. But will you take responsibility for dinner? We said we'd have kedgeree.'

'So, basically, you're going to be out all day?'

'I suppose so, yes. Leave you in peace to watch the football – do the garden, I mean.' They smiled at each other.

She thought she knew exactly what he had in mind, and he hated himself for being the cause of the irony. While Laura was having her wash, he switched on his phone that had been charging overnight on his bedside table. Almost immediately a WhatsApp pinged in.

'*Are you coming?*' It had been sent at 5.13am.

He quickly replied, '*Yes, with you by 11am. Postcode please for satnav.*'

A reply arrived seconds later. '*W11 1PH.*'

He could hear Laura cleaning her teeth. What on earth was he thinking of doing? What was he imagining was going to happen when he got there? He'd spent a couple of hours in her company yesterday, not having seen her for over forty years, and he was now thinking of deceiving Laura and rushing off to London to see her again. How could this possibly be a sensible thing to do? He was being ridiculous.

Laura got dressed and went downstairs for breakfast, and Philip had his wash and shave. He put on his favourite chinos and polo shirt and went downstairs, just as Laura was leaving for church, missal in one hand and handbag full to bursting in the other.

'Have a good day.'

'You too. No need to start cooking until I get back. It only takes half an hour. Will you make sure there's plenty of salad, too?'

'Yup.' Philip noticed that she would be taking his car because hers was blocked in, and he quickly said, 'I'll move my car so you can take yours.'

'No need.'

'No, it's OK, I'll let you out.'

He knew Laura would be perfectly happy to leave his car with him even though she thought he wouldn't actually be using it.

Philip watched her go till she was out of sight, and then rushed back into the house to collect his wallet and his gilet. After checking that everything was off, he took from the larder cupboard a packet of rice and carried it to the car. He quickly punched the postcode into the satnav and set off. Only then did he think in a moment of panic about his clothes: luckily, Laura hadn't thought it strange he had put on smart clothes to do the gardening. *She simply isn't as devious as me*, he thought, and he felt a pang of shame.

The road was clear and he was able to drive quickly, content that the ETA on satnav was suggesting arrival at 10.42. He found himself thinking back to *Macbeth* forty years earlier and how the summer had ended, in a way that even now he could not understand.

17

EARLY AUGUST 1977
AND SIX WEEKS LATER

JERSEY

Two days later, the full run had gone well, Philip very pleased that many of the cast chose to stay to watch the scenes they weren't in rather than chat in the wings or back in the changing room. He was gratified that even though they had more than six weeks till the show he was already almost word-perfect, as indeed was Jane. David had been delighted with the run and in his notes after had commended Philip and Jane in particular, much to their embarrassment. Everyone had decided to go to the pub after the run and they were all in good spirits, with plenty of good-natured ribbing, nobody completely escaping somebody's merciless observation. Philip and Jane were squeezed next to each other on the end of a bench seat and he sensed that neither of them wanted the evening to end. He whispered in her ear, telling her she was beautiful, and was briefly intoxicated by her smell. He then surprised himself when he nuzzled her earlobe, causing her to look at him in mock protest, though her dazzling, smiling eyes could not conceal the small thrill she had felt.

It was last orders and Alan, Donalbain, offered to get them in. Amongst all the jokes about having a *double, double gin and tonic*, Philip said he'd like a pint and Alan looked at him pointedly and said, "'*It provokes the desire, but takes away the performance.*'" Philip looked at Jane, and she held his gaze and smiled. Alison was looking at both of them and smiling, and Philip noticed Jane blush. With everyone else then riveted to another of Alan's anecdotes, Philip saw the flush on her neck and kissed it, again catching her scent and feeling almost overwhelmed by the softness and smoothness of her skin.

Philip declined offers of a lift home for both him and Jane, saying they wanted to go for a walk. He became nervous and excited when she said nothing to contradict his polite refusals.

They had slipped away in the darkness, but once on the road they noticed that the stars and the moon were staging a proud display of celestial magnificence. 'Not much "*husbandry in heaven*" tonight,' Philip said as he took Jane's hand and they started their three-mile walk to Jane's house, Philip at least wishing it were much further. Her hand felt small and he enjoyed wrapping his around it, protecting it, keeping it exclusively for himself. He gently stroked the back of it with his thumb. Her step was a little erratic, he noticed. They were both silent for a while, savouring being alone together, walking slowly to prolong the time it would take to reach Jane's place. Jane accepted Philip's offer to carry her bag. He could see how tired she was.

'Where would you prefer to be now?' he asked.

'Nowhere.'

'Are you happy? I mean really happy?'

'I don't think I have ever felt so contented. It's been a wonderful summer so far. You've been such fun and so kind and I love being with you, "*my dearest partner of greatness*". She leant her head against his arm.

'I wish time would stand still.' He let go of her hand and stopped walking. She stopped as well and turned to face him. 'I can't describe it, but I just know this is the happiest I'm ever going to be in my life. Nothing matters but you and me, and here and now. I love you, Jane.' He had tried, in vain he knew, to invest the words with all the meaning they had for him. He realised he was on the verge of tears, but he couldn't stop. 'I know it sounds stupid, but I swear I have loved you since the moment I first saw you and I know that whatever happens I shall always love you.'

'I love you, too.' She had said it. Said what he had thought she never would. His chest ached as it swelled with joy and pride. 'It has happened gradually,' she continued, leaning on him for support, 'but I knew when you squeezed me on the Ponte Vecchio so tight I almost couldn't breathe that I wanted to be with you because you make me feel special. When we went to dinner at the Bistro a couple of weeks ago and I said thank you for my crab and you said thank you for being here to eat it, I could see how much I meant to you and that made me feel so happy, so warm inside, and so lucky. I don't think I can possibly live up to your expectations of me, Philip, and I don't see how the intensity of your dream can last forever, but here and now I think I must be feeling something like what you're feeling.' He held her close and sensed she was giving herself entirely to his warm protection.

He wanted her to say it again, to end the speech how she had started it, but she didn't, and even at this moment he began to wonder whether or not she had really said it.

The moon was shining down upon the wide stretch of an open field. Neither of them said anything, but they both saw the opening in the hedge and walked through it onto a space a little away from the road and into the shadow of a tall oak standing guard over what Philip could see was an expanse of verdant flatness reaching into the distance, silvered by the moon and stars. He took from her bag the rehearsal blanket and spread it out before helping her to sit down. He kissed her, and tasted the wine she had drunk, mixed with the scent of her perfume and the smell and taste of her mouth. He had thought about this moment so many times, imagining how terrified he would be if it should ever happen, but he undid the buttons of her cardigan and then her blouse without nerves or hesitation. Eyes closed dreamily and her breathing shallow and short, she offered no resistance. As if in some sort of trance, she eased herself out of them, briefly crossing her arms in front of her chest before lying back on the blanket, arms by her side. Her bra shone bright white in the moonlight and he gasped when he saw the perfect curves of her breasts. He did not dare unclasp her bra and, feeling that he had already been granted a glimpse of what he didn't deserve, he leant over her and kissed her. It was slow and luxurious, and he was in another world where nothing existed apart from them and their countless stars. His hand explored her back and shoulders and then moved down to her waist, which seemed absurdly narrow. She stopped breathing for a moment when she realised his hand was starting to move higher, but then she encouraged him by taking his hand and placing it on her breasts and holding it there. She struggled to sit up so that he could reach behind her back to undo her bra. She instinctively moved her arms again to protect her modesty but was quickly and gently persuaded to move them away so that he could see her. He helped her lower herself down onto her back and started gently to curve his hands around her breasts, scarcely believing he was being allowed to see, let alone touch and kiss, such beauty. He thought he could hear something approaching and he held his breath as a car, clearly familiar with the country lanes, made its slow and probably rather drunken way home. He looked down again at the moonlit vision above whom the oak tree rose.

He removed their jeans, urgently and clumsily. Philip knew he was ready and Jane took his hand to between her legs. For a moment, he didn't know what he should do. But then he touched her, and he felt how soft and warm and wet she was. She moaned quietly.

'I want you. Please. Please.'

'But what about…'

'We both…'

'I know, but…'

The palm of her hand.

'Now. Now. Oh, God, God, please.'

He arrived for the last night's performance, buoyed by a glowing review in the local paper and hardly believing how lucky he was to be performing in this play that he loved opposite the girl who had occupied his thoughts for nearly two years and who had been intimate with him in a way that he had never expected even if he had often enough imagined it. He felt life could not get any better. But when he arrived in the communal dressing room – women one end, men the other, with some movable screens in between – and walked directly towards Jane, he was surprised that she got up from her chair and headed to the ladies in a way that he could only think was a deliberate and overt attempt to avoid him. Why? What had he done? What was wrong? He looked at Alison, one of the witches, silently enquiring if she knew what was up with Jane, but he received only a quick shrug of the shoulders as she returned to applying her mascara.

He went back to his own changing station, trying to remain calm but all the while thinking through what had happened over the previous few days, desperately looking for clues to explain Jane's behaviour but not finding any. He remembered their kisses the night before, on stage and off, and was sure she had been as enthusiastic as he had been, their feelings for each other off-stage only helping to suggest the deepest love and passion of the Macbeths on stage. She had disappeared very quickly after the end of the show, but she had given him advanced warning that she would because her sister, Jenny, was going to be in the audience and would need a lift home after and wouldn't want to be kept waiting too long. Philip hadn't minded because he had already arranged the special surprise for her after the last night party, and he could be patient.

He realised that he was getting behind in his preparation – he still had to put on the beard.

He was concentrating hard on the final bits of trimming and saw in his mirror Jane pass behind him. She was obviously avoiding looking at him and he could tell just from her profile that something was bothering her. It didn't look like the plan he had organised to celebrate the last night was going to materialise. Someone came in and said, 'Beginners,' and a number of the cast vacated the space. Philip walked slowly towards her.

'What's wrong?'

'I'm just not feeling great. I'll be OK. Don't worry. We need to concentrate on the show.'

'Is it me? Is it something I've done?'

'No, it's me. I'm sure I'll be fine later. Come on, focus on the show. You'll be on in a minute. Philip, we have to lead this show. It's our responsibility. Time for you to show some respect – some responsibility, I mean.'

Philip looked at her, held her shoulders and leant in to kiss her. She did not move away, but it was clear to him that her response was passive, until she pulled away and turned back to her table to take up her hairbrush. She looked as though she was both on the verge of tears and also trying hard to contain her anger. 'There's no art to find the mind's construction in the face,' he thought, jolting himself into realising that he needed to make his way to the wings.

He got through his first two scenes, but he didn't quite know how because his mind was elsewhere. He was anticipating his first scene with Jane and especially the kiss when he first arrives home.

"'*Great Glamis, worthy Cawdor!*
Greater than both by the all-hail hereafter!
Thy letters have transported me beyond
This ignorant present, and I feel now
The future in the instant.'"

He took her in his arms and tried to kiss her passionately. But he was getting nothing back. Her lips felt cold and dry.

"'*Look like the innocent flower,*
But be the serpent under't. He that's coming
Must be provided for'"

And Philip remembered four months earlier in Florence. Their first kiss. And now this – distant and indifferent, or worse, reluctant, grudging. He felt sick, could taste the acid on the back of his tongue. He almost forgot his line, Jane feeling it necessary to shake him:

"'*We will speak further,*'" he said, and he felt that he couldn't wait for the show to end so that he could confront her to establish exactly what was going on.

He got through the '*If it were done*' soliloquy somehow, but it felt like an out-of-body experience, and then she was back on stage with him. He felt that her taunting and cajoling and tempting had become simply an attack. Where were the love and desire and suggestion that normally could be seen in her eyes? *She is supposed to love me. We are a team.*

"'When you durst do it, then you were a man;
And to be more than what you were, you would
Be so much more the man.'"

Philip was taken back to that Friday rehearsal when they had stayed behind after David had left and had gone through this scene alone on Jane's rug. He remembered how guilty he had felt later, when he realised with great embarrassment that he had been so transported that he had offered nothing in return. He had resolved that it would be different next time and he couldn't wait for the opportunity to arise. He had only had to wait for two days. He knew then that the moment would be the most beautiful of his life.

"'When in swinish sleep
Their drenched natures lie as in a death,
What cannot you and I perform upon
The unguarded Duncan? What not put upon
His spongy officers, who shall bear the guilt
Of our great quell?'"

Philip suddenly realised this was his cue and was jolted out of his memory:

"'Bring forth men-children only!'" he said, and he saw Jane stare through and past him, and she hadn't come back to him when they reached the end of the scene.

18

AUGUST 2018

SUNDAY
EN ROUTE FROM WORCESTER TO LONDON

He had made excellent progress on the M5 and A419 and was now on the M4. The ETA had actually changed for the better; it now said 10.39, but Philip knew that the last part of the journey into London was going to be the slow part, even on a Sunday.

He thought again about how foolish he was being making such a trip. He told himself he didn't really know why he was making it, but actually he knew full well. He had been right on that moonlit night forty years ago when he had thought that whatever happened he would always love her. Why had she been so persuasive, insistent he should visit her, if she didn't share similar feelings or at least feel some kind of need or desire to be with him again? But how could she still have positive feelings after all this time? She had rejected him, after all. You don't have second thoughts after forty years. Although all of the answers to the questions he asked continued to suggest how ridiculous he was being, something still drove him on, and the nearer he got to her home the more excited he became and his desire to know why she wanted so much to see him was almost beginning to drive him mad.

His thoughts returned to the last performance of *Macbeth* and the end of the summer of 1977.

19

SEPTEMBER 1977

JERSEY

"'The queen, my lord, is dead.'"
"'She should have died hereafter.
There would have been a time for such a word"…'

Philip delivered the speech and couldn't stop himself imagining what life would be like if Jane was dead. Yes, he agreed that life would be meaningless, absurd. He knew that their summer together was over. Their scenes together had felt empty and dead. He had tried so hard to put everything into them, but all the stresses had been overdone, the emotions had been faked, his mind had been elsewhere and he felt that Jane's performance had been just as distracted. How could something so perfect suddenly and inexplicably fall apart? What had happened?

They received a very enthusiastic ovation at the curtain call, but as he held her hand for the final full company bow it felt cold and lifeless. She didn't want it to be in his and couldn't withdraw it quickly enough when the lights finally went down. She ran ahead of the rest of the company as they all headed for the changing room and Philip was somehow aware that he wasn't listening to all the good humour and mutual congratulations that the rest of the cast were scattering freely in the best thespian tradition. He was aware that what he had planned for the two of them as a special last-night celebration would not be happening. He felt sick in the pit of his stomach. He wanted to get out of the place as quickly as possible but was desperate for some kind of explanation and knew that he had to be there for the cast party and the presentations and speeches.

He duly made a speech and gave the bouquet of flowers to the make-up lady, Jill, and then watched Jane make a presentation to David, their director. David's speech went on forever, and Philip could see that the whole business was as nauseating for Jane as it was for him. He was also aware that other members of the cast had picked up the vibe and were trying hard, and failing, to hide their awareness that something was clearly amiss with Philip and Jane.

Very soon after the formal part of the proceedings had been completed, Philip saw Jane heading towards the door out of the room. He had to speak to her and rushed over.

'What's the matter? Please tell me. I can't bear this. Tonight was supposed to be a perfect night. I have a special surprise for you.'

'Don't, Philip. I have to go. Please don't try to stop me.'

'You can't just leave without telling me why you're behaving like this. I'm sick with worry about you and about us. I love you, Jane. I need you. You can't just shut me out like this. Suddenly and for no reason.'

'I think we should stop seeing each other. We've had a wonderful summer, but you'll soon be going back to Birmingham and I'll be starting at Durham. We should both make fresh starts.'

'You can't really mean this. I don't want a fresh start. I don't believe you want a fresh start.'

'Yes, I do. I need one.'

'Why, Jane?'

'I just do. It's finished.'

20

AUGUST 2018

SUNDAY
EN ROUTE FROM WORCESTER TO LONDON

He had played the last night's events back in his mind. They were as vivid as if they had been yesterday. He remembered her every facial expression and gesture and tone of voice, and he could still capture at any time the sensations he felt that night when his world changed forever. He questioned again why he was making this journey. He was only twenty-three minutes away from arriving at her home. Should he turn back now? He couldn't. Something so strong compelled him to continue. Even after forty years he dreamt that sometime she would realise her mistake and ask him to come back to her. *And what if she did?* he considered. He realised with a sense of growing alarm that he would not be able to resist.

His mind returned to the end of that summer, and the last time he had seen her before yesterday morning when he had bumped into her on the Green.

21

SEPTEMBER 1977

JERSEY AIRPORT

His brother, Simon, dropped him off. He'd enjoyed showing off to Philip his almost new Ford Capri and Philip himself had been briefly distracted by the car's swanky interior and its power. They'd talked a little about a TV programme they'd both happened to watch the night before, *Genome*, but Philip was grimly uncommunicative, in a hurry to be deposited and to be left alone with his thoughts. He lifted his case out of the boot and grabbed his holdall and said thanks to Simon. They weren't very close. Even before Simon had moved out of their dad's house and into his own flat they had almost been strangers. They didn't really share any interests, but at least Simon made an effort to be friendly whereas Philip offered so little in return.

'Have a good term, then. See you at Christmas.'

'Thanks, Simon. And thanks for the lift,' he managed, before turning on his heels and walking through the double doors into departures.

Fortunately there wasn't much of a queue at check-in and Philip was able to get rid of his suitcase and to settle down with a cup of coffee in an out-of-the-way corner in quick time. He took from his holdall the copy of *Middlemarch* he knew he should already have finished, and felt only mild alarm that he still had four hundred pages to read over the weekend. He knew that if he got into the rhythm he would speed through it, but he was concerned that he wouldn't be able to concentrate because he wouldn't be able to stop thinking about Jane.

He had a school friend who had suffered from depression during sixth form and had been taking strong medication, and he was worried that his own unhappiness could tip over into something more serious.

He was not looking forward to the term ahead. He told himself that he must audition for whatever the drama society was putting on because he needed distractions and needed to meet some new people. He wondered if he would ever have the confidence to make a request to the society to direct a show himself. He knew you had to put in a bid and then go before the committee to explain your ideas and to persuade them to give you the slot. He wondered what he could put on, seeking inspiration by staring at the flight departure board.

'I came to say goodbye and to wish you well for the term.' Jane had appeared in front of him. She looked stunning in a blue silk blouse and one of her favourite Laura Ashley skirts and espadrilles. Philip's immediate thoughts were that he would not catch the plane but instead sit with her drinking tea and coffee for the rest of his life.

'It's so good to see you, Jane. Thank you for coming. And don't worry – I'm not going to make a scene. You look so beautiful and I wish I had a camera and could capture just how lovely you are.'

'I came to say thank you for everything. I will never forget this summer, Philip. I'm sorry that it came to an end, but I knew it had to, and maybe you will understand that too at some time in the future.' He was about to question her, but she continued: 'I have a present for you,' and she dipped into her bag and brought out what was obviously a book, wrapped in simple navy blue tissue paper.

Philip unwrapped it straight away. It was a copy of John Fowles's *The Collector*, and inside the front cover, she had written, 'To Philip, With all my love, Jane X'

'Thank you, Jane. That's a lot better than "All good wishes". Thank you very much.' He moved towards her to kiss her on the cheek, but she turned her face slightly so that their lips met and she held his head in her hands. She then broke away gently and proceeded to walk away, out of departures, without once looking back. Philip had wanted to wish her well for her first term, but it was too late. He wondered if he would ever see her beautiful face again.

22

AUGUST 2018

SUNDAY
LONDON

He was brought out of his reverie by a fast car hooting aggressively and then speeding past him. And then he reflected: she had done the same thing yesterday evening as she'd done forty years ago, transforming a friend's kiss into something more just by turning her head. He considered again just how much power she had over him and he decided he liked the danger of such a situation.

The satnav was indicating that he was only a minute away and it was 10.55. He'd made excellent time and was pleased he would neither have to panic about being late or to kill time by waiting in a lay-by.

'*You have reached your destination.*'

There was a parking space and he slipped into it gratefully, telling himself this was a good omen; he was meant to be there. He realised he didn't know which number she was so texted her to say he had arrived and was waiting outside in the street. Within seconds she appeared on the steps four houses down from his car and waved and smiled at him. A short path of ceramic tiles led to the three steps up to what was a bay-fronted Victorian house forming part of an elegant terrace. It was in immaculate condition.

She led him down a high-ceilinged, long narrow passage, though there was room in it for a console table on which there was a spectacular bright blue and red vase, in which there were at least twenty white roses, and a giant metallic bowl containing sets of keys and other knickknacks. They arrived in a beautiful light and airy kitchen with a large rectangular glass table around which eight chairs fitted with plenty of room to spare. On a large island were a ceramic hob and a huge sink with one of those taps providing instant boiling water. There were audio speakers fitted into the ceiling and Philip thought the system was tuned to Radio 3.

'What a stunning room,' Philip said, noticing the high ceiling, the large ceramic floor tiles, the premium integrated appliances and the high-quality finishes everywhere. He looked through the bi-fold doors at what was clearly a beautifully tended landscaped garden.

'Yes, we like it. I had quite a say in the design, actually. I worked closely with the Harvey Jones lady but even so we managed to get some things wrong – so we should have had more sockets on that wall,' she said, pointing to a long stretch of cabinets and a beautiful piece of black and gold granite with streaks of white and occasional flashes of red. 'It's a lovely space for family life. Unfortunately, more often than not, I'm here alone, rattling around in it.' She held his look and stroked her neck. He looked to see if the red patch had appeared, but it hadn't. 'Coffee?'

'Yes, please.' She moved to another work surface on which was sitting an Italian machine that looked almost as big as the one Philip had seen and heard spluttering away yesterday in Costa.

'Do sit down, Philip.'

'I've been sitting down for the last couple of hours; I'm happy on my feet for a while.'

He strolled around the room, looking at the artwork on the walls. There was a huge oil painting of a beach scene. It reminded Philip of the beach at Plemont in Jersey, but closer inspection told him it was an Irish coastline. He couldn't remember ever looking very closely at oil paintings and he was surprised at how thick the oil was in places. He liked the piece very much. It certainly looked amazing on this wall, its dimensions a perfect match for the dining table, its position naturally catching the light coming in through the doors into the garden and the massive skylight directly and precisely above the table.

'Well, here I am. I'm not quite sure *why* I'm here except that you did invite me.'

'And I love to see you in my home,' she said. Philip thought he remembered Daisy saying something like that to Nick in *The Great Gatsby*, and he found himself briefly contemplating Gatsby himself and the destructive nature of obsession and the impossibility of repeating the past. But he wanted to repeat it. Just once. *Oh, God, please.* He would be better prepared this time.

'We're having roast chicken for lunch. Any good at peeling potatoes?'

'You mean you've dragged me all the way down here to peel spuds?'

'That's obviously the main reason, but there are others too.'

'Such as?'

'Don't be impatient. Potatoes first and then surprises.'

'Surprises?'

'Yes, but potatoes first. For three.'

'You mean this isn't going to be an intimate candle-lit lunch for just me and you in this huge and very light and airy kitchen?'

'The other guest will be here in a few minutes.'

'Is the other guest the real reason I'm here?'

'You could say that, and vice versa.'

'I like cryptic crosswords, and to be honest I'm pretty damn good at the one in *The Telegraph*, but you are confusing me.'

Jane smiled, a little nervously, Philip thought. 'It will soon all become clear,' she said, and she glanced at the huge clock on the wall next to the double doors.

Philip realised he recognised the music; it was the slow movement of Shostakovich's second piano concerto. He started to hum as he peeled but checked himself. He looked at Jane, who was cutting carrots near the sink with an expensive knife, one she'd taken from a sleek block with magnetised fittings. He was about to ask her who the other guest was, but he noticed deep concentration on her face and a steely look in her eyes. He started to feel anxious. What was this all about?

'Jane, why am I here?' She looked at him but didn't reply. 'It can't be that you simply wanted me to peel potatoes for you? Who else is coming? You said your husband is away on business—'

'He is; not back till Wednesday, late. Three more days of freedom.' He saw her close her eyes and shudder.

'Do I know this other guest? Is it someone who by chance knows both of us? Is it a blast from the past?'

'No, you don't know this person.'

'Him or her?'

'Her.'

'Does she know me somehow?'

'No, she doesn't. But I want to introduce her to you.' She paused. 'I had the idea when we bumped into each other yesterday – you and me, I mean.'

'Why?'

'That's far too many potatoes. Let's get them in the pan to parboil. Why don't you sit down? No, better still, go to the fridge over there and open a bottle of wine.'

'I'll happily pour you a glass, but I'm not sure I should drink; I have to drive back this afternoon. I could do with having Laura with me!' He knew what he meant, and he thought Jane probably did, too. He opened the fridge, took out a bottle of New Zealand Sauvignon Blanc and poured Jane a glass.

They both heard a key in the lock, and a woman calling out: 'Hi, Mum. Something smells *gooooood*. I'm starving.'

A striking woman, in her mid-thirties, Philip guessed, walked into the kitchen, threw her arms around Jane, only breaking off the embrace when she noticed the man standing rather awkwardly by the table to her left.

'Ooh, hello,' she said.

'Darling, this is Philip. Philip, this is my daughter, Annie.'

'Very nice to meet you, Annie. Hope you like potatoes.' Philip didn't know where the line had come from, and he realised Annie certainly wouldn't either. Jane relieved them both by explaining how conscientious Philip had been in his contribution to lunch preparations.

'Ooh, may I have a glass of wine, please?' Annie asked when she noticed Jane's glass on the work surface.

'Let me,' said Philip. 'Potato peeler and sommelier. I'm very versatile,' and he poured two glasses, one for Annie and a small one for himself.

'Will you stretch to dishwasher as well later?' Jane asked, still, Philip thought, looking preoccupied.

'Depends on the quality and, indeed, the quantity of the roast potatoes I consume.'

All three of them smiled and looked at each other a little nervously.

'Well, cheers,' Philip said. 'It's nice to be here. Surreal, but nice,' he added, before realising that a *Notting Hill* reference hadn't really been the best idea, because neither Jane nor Annie had recognised the line. 'It's lovely to meet you, Annie. I don't know if you know this, but I've known your mother since schooldays.'

'In Jersey?'

'Yes.'

'I love Jersey. We go there quite often, or used to before Granny died.'

Philip pointed to the large oil painting on the wall. 'Do you know Plemont?' When she nodded and opened her eyes wide, he continued: 'That seascape really reminds me of Plemont, the most beautiful beach on the island, in my opinion.'

'Oh, that's amazing. I've said that to you before, haven't I, Mum, how much I love that beach?' Annie's face was alive with enthusiasm, and Jane nodded happily. 'Apparently Mum almost lost me on Plemont once, when I was about two, wasn't it, Mum?'

'Yes, darling. We were just about to set up base near some rocks, and I turned round to get the rug out of my bag and you must have wandered off because when I turned back round you'd disappeared. I think you were only lost for less than a minute, but it was terrifying. You suddenly reappeared, thank God. I don't think you were permanently scarred by the experience, but I've never forgotten the episode and I still occasionally dream about it.'

'I'm sorry,' Annie said.

'Yes, all your fault, wicked child. Totally thoughtless of you.' Mother and daughter smiled at each other, and Philip found himself enjoying their moment of intimacy and he smiled, too.

Jane walked over to the hob. She drained the potatoes and then tipped them into a baking tray. There was a loud hiss and crackle as the goose fat spat and spluttered around them.

'I hope you're not being too vicious with those potatoes,' Philip said very seriously.

'They'll be the best you've ever tasted,' Jane countered, before slotting the tray into the oven.

'So, how did you and Mum know each other?'

'It's a long story, as they say. Basically we met because of drama; we did plays together. I helped direct a school production of *Twelfth Night* in which your mother played Olivia, and we played opposite each other in *A Streetcar Named Desire* and *Macbeth*.'

'How come you directed *Twelfth Night*?'

'I'd left school and was having what nowadays is called a gap year, and I was invited to help direct the school play by my former English teacher and your mother was in it. This was in 1976, can you believe? That was when we first really met. *Streetcar* was later that year. And the following summer, the summer of 1977, we did *Macbeth* together. After that, your mother started at Durham and we drifted apart, unfortunately.'

Annie was staring at her mother. Her mother was staring at the bottom of her empty wine glass. Philip looked at them both.

'Annie, how about top-ups all round?' Jane asked.

'Yes, OK, hold on,' Annie said, and she stood up and walked out of the room.

Philip saw that Jane was staring at him.

'What?' he asked. She continued simply to look him in the eye. She was obviously not going to speak. 'Why are you staring at me?'

'I also wish the summer of 1977 had gone on forever.'

'It was you who stopped it. I've never fully got over it. Why do you think I'm here, for heaven's sake?'

'Do you remember? At the airport? I said you'd understand one day.'

'I remember exactly what you said. I've replayed the conversation in my mind thousands of times.'

It was her turn to speak, surely, but she was stubbornly silent. Until she said, 'Today's the day.'

He was about to protest that the cryptic comments were really not terribly helpful, but then it hit him deep in his stomach. He looked her in the eye. She didn't flinch. Even at this moment he found himself thinking of Donne's eye image in *The Ecstasy* but chased it away.

'How old is Annie, Jane?'

'She was born on May 1st, 1978.'

His vision became blurred and he felt he might faint. He didn't know if he wanted to kiss her or kill her. This couldn't be happening to him. He was not made for this kind of thing.

'I don't believe it. It can't be true,' he said.

'It is. I swear to God.'

What he had always felt were clichés now became real as he felt the colour drain from his face and thought his legs might crumple underneath him.

'*I want you. Please. Please.*'

'*But what about…*'

'*We both…*'

'*I know, but…*'

'*Now. Now. Oh, God, God, please.*' The palm of her hand. She had. She had wanted him. *Oh, God.*

'Philip?'

'Yes. Sorry. Oh, God. Why didn't you tell me? You've let me live for forty years not knowing! And what about Annie? What does she know?'

'She only knows that I loved her father.'

'Yes, so much so that you kept his daughter from him for forty years.'

'And I would have kept the secret for ever if I hadn't bumped into you yesterday on the heath.'

'On the Green. So you'd have allowed me to go to the grave, you'd have allowed yourself to go to the grave... What about Annie, would you ever have told her if we hadn't met yesterday?'

'I don't know, Philip. It hasn't been easy for me, you know. I loved you that summer and I didn't want it to end how it did. It broke my heart, too, you know. When I left you at the airport you couldn't see the tears running down my face as I walked away from you. But my mother had a solution, and I couldn't see any other way.'

In spite of his confusion and his anger, he was feeling an overwhelming sympathy for her, and he stood up and wondered if he should hold her. He saw her start to sob quietly and he gently took her head in his hands. He wiped her tears away with his thumbs, making her convulse even more.

'Please hold me,' she said. But he didn't. He closed his eyes and inhaled deeply. When he opened them he saw Annie standing in the doorway. She was pale and looked completely shattered; she had been crying and was shaking. She looked at him and then slowly walked towards them both, before changing her mind. The three of them stood still and in silence, no one knowing where to look or what to say.

'Do you think those potatoes need basting?' he asked after some time, and both Jane and Annie smiled, almost laughed, statues coming back to life. They were both smiling and crying: *Sunshine and rain at once*, he reflected. And then he realised he was doing exactly the same, and shaking, too.

When Annie sat down, Philip and Jane joined her. He sensed that both he and Jane wanted to speak, but he did not know what they would say. He instinctively felt that Annie should decide what should happen or be said next. He knew Annie was finding it hard to look directly at him, but he desperately wanted to look closely at her, to examine a face he didn't know even though it was his flesh and blood.

Eventually, Annie spoke. 'Any chance you might share a few details about your secret, Mum?' *She's trying so hard to be brave*, Philip thought. He looked at Jane.

'*I hate to seem inquisitive*, as Jack Worthing would say, but do you mind if I listen in?' His request did not produce a smile. Jane held her hands as if in prayer in front of her face, her index fingertips gently pinching the flesh between her nostrils.

She explained how she had gone to Durham at the start of October 1977, knowing she was pregnant with Philip's child. Her mother had suggested that if Jane could manage the first term on her own she would take a house in Durham from January and be there for her for the rest of the course, helping her during the later stages of the pregnancy and when the child was born.

'It was a terribly difficult time, of course, especially during the first year, but after the birth, strangely the situation became easier.' She was dabbing her eyes with her hanky. 'My mother was wonderful. She knew who the father was without asking and she never introduced your name into the conversation, Philip, only talking about you if I mentioned your name. She never blamed you, but she was adamant I shouldn't tell you because that would not only complicate my life even more but also yours in a way that couldn't possibly help anyone.' She saw he was about to interrupt. 'Don't, Philip, please. This is hard enough as it is. I wanted to tell you. I nearly did at the end of the summer and I wrote to you so many times without posting the letter because I knew it should be done face to face. She never reproached me for being so naïve and irresponsible, or you, and she was so patient when I was at my lowest. I was so miserable and frightened, you know.' She sniffed and just managed to stop herself sobbing. 'I think she actually enjoyed the new and unexpected responsibility.'

Annie and Philip continued to listen in silence, both still in a state of shock, Annie still so pale. Annie rested her hand on his, and he found himself taking it and comparing how it felt with the cold hand of her mother at the final curtain call. But then she seemed to have second thoughts and withdrew it.

'I don't see how you were able to keep it a secret. How did people not find out? Does anybody else know?' Annie asked, her thoughts exactly the same as her father's.

'It was only really difficult at first. Mum and I stayed away from Jersey during the summer vacation after you were born, spending time in mum's rented house in Durham, but we also went up to the Isle of Skye, and we stayed there for most of August and September, away from everyone.'

Philip looked at her telling the story and wondered if she was reciting the letter she said she had written so many times but never sent.

'We had only one visitor, the only other person who knows: your Auntie Jenny.' She looked at Annie, and Philip thought Annie was wondering how Jenny had also managed to keep the secret.

'She knew nothing until she joined us and discovered there were three of us there already. She knew straight away who the father was, but she was sworn to secrecy and she has kept her promise for forty years. My dad knew, of course. He never reproached me either.

'When I returned to Durham at the start of the next academic year, those people who knew I had a child were really not interested in discovering the identity of her father. I made it clear anyway that the subject was simply not up for discussion and actually people showed a remarkable willingness to respect my wishes for privacy. For once I was so pleased not to be the centre of attention. I wasn't the only student mother, after all. I thought and always intended the secret would remain a secret forever because, well… Anyway, Mum has also died now, and when Jenny and I go nobody on earth would know. You, my darling,' she said, looking at Annie, 'have always accepted what I have always told you: "Your father is someone I loved very much, but he disappeared from my world." Except yesterday I saw him for the first time in forty years, and everything I had believed and intended suddenly changed. And I mean suddenly.'

She looked at Philip. 'When you quoted from *Lear* in Costa, suddenly I just knew. I had to hold back the tears and I suddenly accepted what I had really known all along, that the two of you deserved… deserve to know. And I knew that this was the one chance there would be. Both time and place do now adhere.'

She looked at Philip and placed both of her hands on his. He looked at her, seeing again the girl who had provided him with such intense joy and also such heartbreak, all in the course of the same summer. He felt an acute desire to return to 1977, a rack-stretching, aching longing to be back in that summer. If only he could have again one day, even just an hour of that precious time. If only he could return to the bridge. The blanket. Her face under the oak. The wishing was hurting his chest. He found himself back in departures, remembered the last night of the play, and he clenched his fists and closed his eyes tight so that she wouldn't be able to look into his eyes to tell him it was over. When he forced himself to open his eyes, he turned to face Annie, and she held his look. He remembered the car in the lane. Jane's hand. She *had* guided him. He thought he saw the hint of a smile in one corner of Annie's mouth. He smiled at her, lopsided again, he imagined. She continued to hold his look briefly but then looked down at her hands.

More silence. Intense, heavy silence. Philip noticed the quiet hum of the oven behind him.

'So, what now?' Annie looked at them both. She wiped what remained of her tears from her cheeks and he noticed some colour had returned to her face. He liked the way she appeared to be trying to move forward. He wanted a daughter with spirit, who wouldn't sulk and mope, and he felt his chest expand with something that felt like pride and he had to fight back the tears that were threatening to start again.

'I don't know,' Jane said. 'We need time to think; there's no need to rush into anything. There are still only four people who know.'

'How do you keep a secret like this? I just can't imagine how you have managed – for all this time. Half a lifetime! A whole lifetime,' Philip added, looking at Annie. He heard his voice crack. Annie looked at him again, and he knew there was warmth in her eyes. Eyes like her mother's.

He was overwhelmed. He thought that she could very easily reject him, thought that this would perhaps be the more likely response to what she had just discovered. But she was looking at him, her face telling him silently that she could see there might be a future for them. Give it time. He felt it already. '*Sometimes, there's God, so quickly,*' he thought, and he silently upbraided himself for living his life through literature, before thinking that his life had now become stranger than fiction. And then he couldn't stop himself: "'*If this were played upon the stage now I would condemn it as an improbable fiction,*'" he said, but, to his surprise, Jane didn't pick up the reference and neither did Annie.

'I promise to play a more active part in your life from now on,' he offered, sniffing and wiping his nose with his hanky to try to show that his composure had returned. When his attempt at humour actually produced a smile in both of them, he thought he'd try another line: 'I bet those potatoes are nice and crisp by now.'

Annie and Jane played with their food, but Philip managed to clear his plate. 'I'm not going to let a tiny little surprise spoil my lunch,' he said. 'It's what I drove all the way from Worcester for, after all.' For much of the time while they ate, Jane told Annie about 1976 and 1977, with Philip contributing occasionally, usually to make fun of himself. Jane's account included one or two details Philip had forgotten, but mostly it was just as he remembered it, and he was happy that what she said confirmed that his memories were real and not some fiction that imagination, dreams and time had combined to deceive him into thinking had happened.

Jane got up from the table and left the room.

'I want to know about your family, Philip... Dad,' Annie said.

'Philip's fine, Annie.'

He told her briefly about his work, about Laura and her two new half-brothers, and she said she wanted to meet them, but he could not see how such a scenario could be arranged yet so told her that there was no rush, and was relieved when Jane came back in.

'What do you think of this?' she said, handing Annie a photograph.

'Oh my God,' Annie said, her hand flying to her mouth. 'You're both so young. You look very beautiful, Mum. Good beard, Philip!'

Philip looked at the photograph and recognised it straight away; he also had a copy of it somewhere. There they were, as Macbeth and Lady Macbeth in act 1 scene 7; the dress rehearsal.

Jane said, 'There is a third person in that picture. Not a witch, or hallucination, or a ghost. Guess who it is.'

Annie briefly looked totally nonplussed; there was clearly nobody else there. But then she understood and slowly shook her head and smiled.

'Yes, darling. You would have been about six weeks old.'

Annie placed the photograph on the table in front of her, cupped her face in both hands and stared down at it. Both Jane and Philip looked at her in silence, before deciding at exactly the same moment to look at each other. Jane's eyes burnt into him, making him want to kiss her, making him want to kiss again the beautiful nineteen-year-old with whom he had fallen in love. Annie looked up before slowly looking back down at the photo. Philip looked at Jane and he realised his expression must have told her he had gone back forty years.

'It wasn't to be,' Jane said.

'It could have been, though, couldn't it?' Annie said. 'Everything could have been different. It could all have been so much better.'

'You can't know how it would have turned out, Annie,' her mother insisted. 'We might not have finished our degrees. Anything could have happened. We might have stayed together for a short while, for a time after you were born, but it could easily have ended at any moment.'

'I would never have ended it, Jane. You know that, don't you?'

'Oh, Philip, you're a hopeless romantic. I was never real to you but always some kind of dream. You thought I was something I wasn't, you thought—'

Philip interrupted her: 'Why am I here now? I'm here now because I was right all those years ago. I said I would always love you whatever happened, and I *have* always loved you. I have never stopped loving you. You have never been far from my thoughts. I love you now. I love you now with the intensity I felt as a nineteen-year-old. When I caught sight of you yesterday, it wasn't a little twinge of nostalgia I felt. It was a burning love for you still. I almost choked with love and pain thinking about what I had once had and what I had lost. And now you tell me I am the father of your child and my heart is bursting. And I am supposed to be watching the football on the TV in Worcester and preparing a meal for my wife. We have two children who have been the pride and joy in our lives for thirty years. But I am here in your house with you and with my forty-year-old daughter whose life I know nothing about. So, Jane, please tell me what I'm supposed to do now.'

There was silence in the room.

'You can't now unknow the truth,' Jane said.

'I don't want to unknow it. I love the truth. But I now have two families, and having spent the last forty years grateful that my life has been very happy if somewhat conventional, I now find that my life is almost unbelievable and I don't know what to do.'

Philip got up and paced around the kitchen. He looked at his watch. Panic set in immediately.

'Oh, God. I can't bear to do this, but I have to go. I'll come back. I'll come back later in the week. Just let me work something out. I'm coming back soon, I swear. I swear. Oh, this is unbearable. But I have to go back home now and be there when Laura gets in.' He wanted to hold Annie tight, and then hold Jane. He wanted to kiss her and to feel her hand in his again.

But he turned to go and refused to look back because he knew he couldn't risk it. He heard Jane's voice: 'I want you to come again, Philip. Please come back.' He waited for three more words. But they didn't come. He let himself out, got into his car and started it up. Somehow he managed with shaking hands to set the satnav and drove away, mouthing, 'I'll be back. Love you,' to the two women standing on the doorstep.

They watched his car move into the distance and he didn't see Jane turn to Annie, nod slowly and smile.

23

AUGUST 2018

SUNDAY
EN ROUTE FROM LONDON TO WORCESTER

Philip wanted to speak to both Annie and Jane and several times had been near to using his car phone to call Jane's mobile. But he did not know what else could be said and he realised that speaking to her now would only cause them both more pain and distress. He knew it would not take very much for him to turn the car round and to go back.

But he had to get to Worcester. He knew he needed to be home, and the traffic getting out of London was causing him to panic about how long the journey would take him. Every traffic light was against him and every time he moved into what he thought would be a quicker lane he was thwarted. It took an hour to travel the dozen or so miles to the M4 and even then a lane was closed, which meant he couldn't just put his foot down.

What, if anything, would he say to Laura? He was sure he shouldn't say anything yet. Nothing at all, at least until he had seen Jane and Annie again and tried to agree a way forward. But what possible way forward was there? He knew that most problems could be solved given time and a clear head, but this one was different. Or was it? Why not just tell her the full story? He had done nothing wrong. There was just a part of his life before he had met Laura that had suddenly resurfaced. Nothing about the last thirty-eight years had changed. The past had caught up and the future would be different, but that was no reflection on everything he had experienced and shared with Laura. But what would the future be? He simply couldn't work it out. He knew he couldn't unknow what he had just found out and, anyway, he didn't want to unknow it. He wanted everything.

He kept stealing looks at his phone, picking it up from the passenger seat and checking to see if a message had appeared. But there was nothing. His heart pumped furiously when he only just managed to avert colliding with the car on the inside lane. *That's one way to sort things*, he reflected. But the thought of his life ending now sickened him: he couldn't bear the idea of losing his family, his families, and never seeing them again.

He knew his journey would last another hour when he left the M4 and joined the Cirencester road; a little less, perhaps, if he really went for it and the traffic cooperated. *Would Laura be back from visiting her mum? Had she taken her out for tea?*

When he arrived on the drive he saw Laura's car, went into a mild panic and prayed that she hadn't been home for long. He walked into the house and immediately noticed the doors into the back garden were open. She was on the patio, sorting out some celeriac, some misshapen courgettes and some scruffy green beans, produce he guessed Angela must have given her.

'How long have you been back?' he asked, anxiously.

'I've just got back now. Where have you been?'

'I had to go to the stores to get some rice for the kedgeree. Oh, damn, left it in the car after all that.'

'Oh, sorry. Thought we had plenty. I'm going for a shower. And I'm very much looking forward to a glass of wine when I come down, with plenty of ice in it.'

He smiled at her. 'Me, too. I've had a busy time as well, you know.'

'Oh yes, it's exhausting watching football, isn't it?'

Laura smiled, too, and then headed inside. He waited a minute, then went back out to the car and collected the rice from the front seat, pleased that Laura saw him retrieving the packet from their bedroom window.

He decided he wouldn't wait for Laura to finish showering to crack open a bottle. There was a nice bottle of white Burgundy in the fridge and he poured himself an enormous glass. "*Here's to my love*," he said half aloud before taking a big gulp. But straight away he realised that the words were Romeo's; he was drinking the fatal poison he had bought from the apothecary. He swallowed some more in an attempt to change the subject. He suddenly thought that he didn't know the results of the football matches he had supposedly been watching so he consulted his phone, then took his glass of wine outside and headed for the patio at the top of the garden. He reflected on what had happened in the last day and a half and how his world had suddenly and irrevocably changed.

He saw Laura appear through the patio doors and head towards him. She hadn't poured herself a glass of wine and clearly expected him to do the honours. He remembered he had been happy to be waiter, sommelier indeed, earlier in the day and he was happy to be so again now. Besides he was already in need of a top-up.

'Your drink will be with you shortly,' he said as they crossed on the lawn.

'Have we got any crisps?'

'I'll have a look.'

He felt absolutely drained of energy but thought better of complaining of weariness to someone who had probably had a very stressful time with her poor mum.

'No crisps, I'm afraid, but some cashews. Cheers!'

'Cheers. Thank you. Mmm, that's nice. What is it?'

'It's a Burgundy. Three pounds off at Tesco.'

Philip sat back and closed his eyes. He felt so tired, but his mind wouldn't slow down and he was already fretting about how he could get back to London in the next few days. Maybe they could meet halfway. A walk in the Cotswolds? He felt dreadful that he would be deceiving Laura, but he knew it was simply too early to tell her anything. He told himself again that he had nothing to be ashamed of, but even so he hated being dishonest or secretive and knew instinctively that by keeping quiet he was embarking on something that wouldn't end well.

'How's your mum?'

'She's OK. She still knows me, and she remembers such strange things in such amazing detail, but she keeps on repeating them. I swear she told me ten times about the time when I bit the doctor's finger. It's so sad. She has no idea who you are, or the boys. Anyway. I also brought home a whole big ice-cream tub full of tomatoes Angela gave me. It's in the upstairs fridge. We mustn't get any from Tesco this week; they'll only go to waste.'

They passed a very amicable evening, finishing the bottle of Burgundy as they ate the kedgeree with some smoked halibut. They shared a bar of Lindor. They searched Sky Movies and Netflix for a good film without success but then found themselves getting interested in an episode of *Fake or Fortune* about a work by Toulouse-Lautrec. After the news,

Laura said they should do the washing up, but Philip said he would do it in the morning.

Laura would probably carry on reading until quite late, but he managed just a few pages before he gave up, knowing he wasn't actually taking anything in, switched out his bedside light, turned onto his side and soon fell asleep.

He found himself in a biblical land where he was the king with a wise man's beard, except it was black. The land was Bohemia or Sicilia. Two women were summoned to his court, both of them widows of the same husband. They brought with them three children, all daughters, two of them three and six, the other aged nine. They had been ordered to appear before the king, who would choose one of the children to be brought up in his palace with every luxury that power and privilege could provide. Both widows begged the king not to choose their progeny, saying that they needed their mother. The king was in no mood to be merciful, though. He drew a chalk circle on the palace floor and ordered that the children be made to lie down feet first inside the circle with their waists resting on the circle's perimeter. He took the legs of the first child, named Miranda, and ordered her mother to take her hands. He decreed that there would be a tug-of-war and whoever succeeded in pulling the child, either fully inside or fully outside the circle, would take the child to live with them forever. Her mother quickly gave in to the king's brutal force, fearing for her daughter's safety. The same procedure was repeated for her second child, Grusha. Again, the mother quickly released her child's hands. The process was repeated with the second mother and her child, Perdita. Again the king was not prepared to let the child go, and the mother released her. The mother's face was covered in tears, and showing no fear of the king's complete authority, she confronted him, saying, 'I have raised my child for all these years on my own and now you snatch her from me. You do not understand what love is.'

The king was immediately wracked with shame and filled with compassion, and ordered that the trials should happen again. This time, he offered no resistance to each of the mothers and said, '*Upon my head they placed a fruitless crown. Let them be thine, for we have no such daughters.*' He sat down and silently wept as he watched the two mothers and their daughters get into his car and drive away in the direction of France.

Bright car headlights swept across his bedroom wall through the curtains. He had woken up to hear one of the neighbours arriving home. His alarm clock said 00.34.

He was surprised he had fallen asleep so quickly but not surprised at all that he now found himself wide awake, soaking with sweat and with a head filled with scorpion thoughts. He contemplated getting up, switching on his phone and going downstairs to see if Jane had texted, but knew that he could do nothing useful overnight so resolved to try to relax, to encourage all the tension to seep out of his body and to try to go back to sleep. He imagined listening to the meditation app on his iPad and breathed in and out slowly and deeply. On a number of occasions he felt he was so close to losing consciousness, only to be snapped away from the edge. He decided he wouldn't turn over but try again, still lying on his back. It didn't seem to be working, but he refused to panic and concentrated hard on the slow and deep inhalations and exhalations. After a long while he was briefly aware that he was close to sinking and then he was aware of nothing at all.

When he awoke and immediately saw his bedside clock reading 07.17 he was relieved that he must have slept long and deeply. He thought briefly that he had dreamt everything that had happened over the last few days, but his feelings of excitement and fear told him it was real. He slipped out of bed into his waiting slippers and went downstairs to make a cafetière of coffee, washing, drying and putting away the kedgeree pan while waiting for the kettle to boil.

24

AUGUST 2018

TUESDAY
WORCESTER

Philip was laying the table while Laura washed the pak choi.

'Not the Shakespeare place mats, Philip, please. The raffia ones are much nicer. And the wine glasses without stems, please. And the white napkins – in the drawer with the mats.'

He was feeling slightly apprehensive, as he always did when they were entertaining. Laura was calmness personified: 'It's just a casual supper, Philip. How many times have Rosemary and Jack been here? We're not trying to impress. We're having a meal with our friends.' She smiled at him, and he knew she was right, of course. He wished he had her temperament: no extremes; just kind good humour. Self-effacing. But also strong and resilient. Someone he had always needed. His Horatio: never *'passion's slave'*.

'Please stop looking at your phone, Philip. You need to finish the table and then please will you make sure the chairs outside are clean?'

The landline rang. *Surely not?* he thought. *She wouldn't, would she?*

'I'll get it,' he said.

'It's all right. I'm there.' He watched her pick up and held his breath even though he knew it could be one of any number of callers. He saw her frown and felt his stomach contract. He wanted to catch her eye, but she had turned around and was looking out into the garden. He needed to be certain it wasn't Jane, so he walked round her to look at her, hands out to seek a mouthed answer to his mimed enquiry. She shook her head and pointed to the kitchen, mouthing instructions that he should wash the mushrooms.

'Oh, Sarah, I'm very sorry. That is so sad. No, no, please don't worry about work at all. You must take as long as you need. And I'll be cross with you if you come in at all this week. You must look after your poor mum.'

Philip was feeling relieved but also concerned for Sarah. He looked at Laura for confirmation of what he was suspecting. She nodded reassuringly at him but pointed him in the direction of the kitchen, and she followed him in, going to the fridge to take out the bag of mushrooms. She pointed to the sink.

'Next Monday? Where will it happen? Oh, that's a beautiful church.' She was nodding thoughtfully. 'Oh, it's lovely there. How have you managed to make arrangements so quickly? You've done brilliantly. Yes, I can imagine. They say it's good to keep busy, don't they?'

She had taken a pen from the jar and was writing instructions for him on the pad: *'Make sure really clean; cut v thin slices.'*

'OK, of course. Yes, you must. That's absolutely fine. And, Sarah, please ask me to do something if I can help in any way. I'm sure, but even so.' There was quite a long period of silence while Laura simply nodded in response to what she was hearing. She encouraged Philip to slice the mushrooms even more thinly. 'Yes, yes, of course. Take care, Sarah. Bye.'

'Her father?' Philip enquired.

'Massive heart attack. Only seventy-one.'

'Are you her boss?'

'No. She works in Richard's department, but she knows me better than him. He's not easy to talk to, either. Poor Sarah. And her poor mum. It was so sudden. We must enjoy life while we can.' She breathed in, audibly and slowly. 'Come on. They'll be here in a few minutes. I'll finish these. Will you check outside?' He nodded slowly and made his way outside.

No new texts. *We must enjoy life while we can.*

'Philip, they're here,' she called.

'Coming.' He quickly finished arranging the last garden chair and hurried inside, and they both greeted Jack and Rosemary. Wine, white and red, chocolates, and a beautiful pot plant were handed over, all contained in an exceedingly smart laminated carrier bag with ribbons attached.'

'Oh, Rosemary. Why have you brought all of this? You shouldn't have, really,' Laura said as she took out the plant and left Philip to deal with the bottles. She continued: 'This is a bird's nest fern, isn't it?'

'Oh, I don't know. I just thought it looked so lovely and healthy,' Rosemary said.

'It does, doesn't it? I'm going to put it in our en suite because these things love a humid environment. We've got a hanging planter in there that will be just perfect. Ooh, thank you.' And she gave Rosemary a big hug.

Philip had taken the bottle of Petit Chablis, Jack's favourite, out of the fridge and was pouring four glasses. 'Come on, let's take these outside.'

It was still so warm and the air was absolutely still. They all walked slowly around the garden, chatting about their children and then inevitably about the start of the new term. Jack and Rosemary had recently returned from a holiday in Corsica and were suggesting that all four of them should go together next summer, to celebrate Philip's retirement. Jack had taught with Philip for over thirty years and he said he would probably do just another three years before he retired, to spend the rest of his life playing golf every day.

'That suits me,' Rosemary said. 'I wouldn't want you under my feet at home all day.'

Jack turned to Laura and said, 'You heard that, didn't you?'

'Heard what?' Eyes wide, raised shoulders and big expansive gesture. And a smile.

Jack turned to Philip: 'So it's not just my wife who's selectively deaf then?'

Jack proceeded to dominate the conversation. He was effortlessly witty and though Philip was sometimes the butt of his kind-hearted humour, more often than not self-deprecation was his style, and then when Rosemary quipped at his expense he made a great play of being outraged. Philip envied Jack his gregarious confidence.

Top-ups all round later, Laura called them in to eat. She was such a good hostess, Philip thought, for the simple reason that she was herself; as she'd said, she wasn't trying to impress and was completely natural. The only thing he wasn't happy to let her do was load the dishwasher.

Jack was showing them photos on his phone, of Corsica and then of their grandson, Billy. In a number of the shots, he was sitting proudly in his plastic red car, a huge smile on his chocolate pudding-covered face. Both Jack and Rosemary were clearly doting grandparents and immensely proud of him.

'Just you wait until you have one like this,' Rosemary said. 'Do you think either Tom or George is likely to get married soon?'

'I don't think so,' Laura said, a smile on her face managing to suggest both contentment but also just a little disappointment. 'They're clearly not in any hurry. Having much too much fun as it is, so why change anything? It will be nice, though, when it happens. It only seems like yesterday that we adopted them. Nearly twenty-five years ago. Where has the time gone?'

'Fortunately none of us has changed at all in that time,' Jack quipped. He looked at Philip: 'You looked about sixty even then.'

'The difference is that I feel it now.'

'Don't we all, mate!'

Some time later their taxi arrived and Philip and Laura waved them off. 'We'll pick up the car in the morning,' Jack called. 'Lovely evening. Thank you both.'

They went back inside and started to tackle the washing up. Philip felt inexpressibly weary, but Laura was still bright and busy. He thanked her for the lovely food and promised he would take responsibility for the cooking next time.

'We'll do it together,' she said, smiling. He looked at her back as she was washing a last saucepan and knew he was so lucky, and really didn't deserve to be.

His phone had been vibrating persistently all evening.

25

THURSDAY

For three days, Jane had been texting Philip, urging him to visit again. *'I feel lonely here on my own.' 'I was so happy being with you on Saturday and again on Sunday.' 'I want to be with you again. It won't be a wasted journey, Philip! XX,'* she had written, tempting and tantalising. *'I have something for you.'* He had tortured himself speculating about her meaning. *'I'll be a "most kind hostess".'* He recognised the echo, the allusion and felt himself being again in the palm of her hand. His desire to see her again was intense and obsessive, keeping him awake at night and then waking him when he had eventually fallen asleep, but he had been unable to manufacture the opportunity and he couldn't bear to lie to Laura again. But on the Wednesday night, late, Jane had telephoned him. Laura had just gone up to bed and Philip had told her that he was just going to have a stroll up the garden before joining her.

He was finishing a glass of red on the patio, staring at a moth repeatedly flying into the outside light. He thought of Blanche Dubois and a book of criticism about the play he had really enjoyed, *The Moth and the Lantern*. The moth was a wonderful symbol for Blanche – attracted as she was to the very thing that destroys her. And then his phone had rung. Jane was tearful, pleading with him to meet her tomorrow when she was going to be in Oxford with Annie visiting her sister, Jenny. She said Bill was drunk when he came in and she was afraid; she was always afraid of him when he'd been drinking. Philip had agreed to meet her, his mind darting and his heart starting to race in anticipation. Shortly after saying he'd be there, he remembered it was A level results day tomorrow. For once, he'd have to give it a miss. He didn't need to be there. He had no official responsibilities. He would find out the results later. He recalled his conversation on Saturday with James. Eighteen years old. Behave yourself, he'd told him.

He poured himself another glass of merlot, emptying the bottle, savouring every sip as he anticipated the prospect of seeing her again and tasting her lips once more. He saw an image of Bill King in his mind's eye. A bully. A man who thought money was power. His enemy. The antagonist.

He decided as he climbed the stairs to tell Laura that he was going to Oxford to meet Jane again. She was going to be there principally to visit Jenny, who was an English don at Trinity, and she had suggested Philip join them. He explained how they had exchanged mobile numbers when they had met on Saturday. He said that he knew Jenny, Jane's sister, even if he hadn't seen her either since those days back in Jersey. He knew the invitation had to be extended to Laura as well and he pretended that he wanted her to go with him, but she said she really didn't want to spend half a day on the train in order to pass time with people she didn't know and, anyway, she didn't want to cramp his style as they all reminisced. He assured her she'd enjoy their company and she'd certainly enjoy Oxford, but she said she was happy to potter at home and to spend time in the garden, having neglected it a little recently because visiting her mum had been her priority.

He didn't sleep. He wanted to hold Jane in his arms. He kept seeing her lips and feeling her hand in his. He kept picturing this thug with a permanent five o'clock shadow and an ugly mouth.

The following morning, having checked again that Laura genuinely wouldn't mind if he went, Philip set off to drive to College Green where he would park and from where he would walk to Foregate Street station. Not Milford Junction. He was relieved that he was unaccompanied but was also feeling very uneasy about his equivocation. Laura didn't deserve this and though he hadn't actually lied to her, he was, of course, not telling her the full story. He told himself that somehow the situation would resolve itself in time and that he would not allow himself to get involved in anything that could do lasting damage to Laura and their relationship. But he also knew that he was already deeply involved in something that couldn't just go away. He couldn't unknow the truth. *What's done cannot be undone*, he thought, and he didn't know whether or not he enjoyed the irony. He was pleased when he was able to park the car without bumping into a colleague or a former pupil.

He occupied his thoughts during the train journey with *The Telegraph* crossword on his iPad. He rattled through it and was mildly, if briefly, gratified that a couple of other passengers had noticed. He particularly enjoyed '12 *across: Thirstier Swedes when drunk become fatal temptresses (3, 5, 7)*'. They passed through Moreton-in-Marsh and he remembered playing cricket there once and the lovely picnic lunch Laura had prepared.

Soon the train was pulling into Oxford and he went over in his mind what he had resolved to say to Jane. He was going to suggest that they both tell their partners the full story. He was going to tell Laura he had driven to London on Sunday and had been introduced to his forty-year-old daughter, someone who was born before he had even met Laura. He was going to apologise for deceiving her, explaining that Jane had persuaded him to go by saying she had something to show him. Nothing was going to change. There was simply going to be another person in his life and he hoped that in time she would be accepted by Laura and their boys. Jane had obviously been an incredibly important person in his past, but that had been over forty years ago and he hoped that they could be friends again now that they had become reacquainted, and that Laura would accept her, embrace her even, as a friend as well. This seemed reasonable, he thought. But he also knew that this proposed confession was still not completely honest. It made no mention of his current thoughts about Jane, and how her reappearance had brought back intense feelings over which he seemed to have very little control. He closed his eyes and shook his head, and then told himself he was prepared to trust Time to untangle the knot.

He had walked past the Saïd Business School, proceeded down George Street and was walking along Broad Street to where they had arranged to meet, outside the Sheldonian Theatre. It was nearly 10.50am and starting to get very hot. No blotches on his shirt yet, he was pleased to notice. He was ten minutes early but knew he could happily spend time in Blackwell's. He would buy Laura a novel and would see if he could top up his own Shakespeare library. He walked past The White Horse pub, and remembered having lunch in there once when he had come to Oxford with a colleague in the English department and the school librarian, ostensibly to buy books for the school, but really it was a jolly to celebrate the start of examination leave for the public exam candidates and, with lighter timetables, a little bit of freedom for the staff.

Although most of the students had gone down for the summer, the city was still busy with young people and hundreds of tourists. He slipped into Blackwell's and immediately noticed a new Kate Atkinson that he picked up, and, having read the front and back covers, he took it to the counter. He paid for it, and, having decided to give Shakespeare a miss, walked back out. Opposite, on the other side of the road, he saw the three of them, hand in hand, looking terribly serious. Annie caught sight of him and smiled, nervously he thought. He crossed the street. He did not know if he should embrace her and felt he could see the same indecision on her face. Jane smiled, and gently stroked his chest. He turned to Jenny, arms outspread.

'Stellaaah!' He made to go down onto his knees.

'Oh, don't do that. If your knees are anything like mine, you'd never get back up. And I think you'd struggle to carry me these days.'

'I struggled to carry you then!'

'Not a particularly chivalrous observation, Philip.'

'No, no, no. You were as light as a feather, but I was pathetically weak.'

'Too late, I'm afraid. The damage is done. Anyway, I don't imagine Jane wants to be reminded of *Streetcar*.'

'Why not?' Philip asked.

'Well, you remember the reviews, don't you?' Jenny said. 'High praise for you and me; only moderate commendation for big sister. And big sister also didn't like the reviewer's suggestion that it might have been interesting if she and I had swopped parts.'

'Now there's a thought,' Philip said, glancing at Jane, who didn't seem entirely amused. 'Well. Anyway. It's really lovely to see you, Jenny. It's been a few years, hasn't it?'

'Who's counting?' she said. 'You look well, by the way. Now, I've already explained this to Jane and Annie, and I know this is going to seem abominably rude, but I have to rush off. An unscheduled meeting. But I had to say hello before leaving the three of you to it. However, I'm guessing I'll maybe see you again before too long. Proper catch-up then, OK? Bye, Annie. Bye, Sis. Love you both.' She turned and walked away, turning back to blow a kiss first at Annie, and then at Jane. 'And, Philip?'

'Yes, Jenny?'

'Be careful! She hasn't changed. And I'm sure you remember what she was like!'

'Can't think what you mean.' Jenny smiled back at him and hurried away. He turned to Jane and Annie: 'You two aren't also going to vanish into thin air, are you?'

As if in reply, Jane took one of his arms and marched him across the street and into The White Horse, Annie close behind. His immediate thoughts were that the inside looked like a pub he'd seen in episodes of *Morse*. There was a small round table in the corner and they were able to claim it without any competition from another customer. Philip said he'd go to the bar, but Annie insisted she was going, saying she would get them all a glass of white wine.

As Philip and Jane sat down, he noticed her hand looked swollen and he took hold of it to inspect. She turned to face him, and he saw that her right cheek was bruised under the thin layer of make-up she'd applied. His mind went back to the tearful phone call the night before.

'How did this happen?' he asked, gently stroking her face. He felt himself becoming angry even before she replied.

'Oh, it's nothing.'

'Yes, it is. And what happened to your hand, as well?'

'Nothing has happened to my hand,' she said.

'Yes, it has,' he insisted, and as he took it again he noticed her wince and then try to smile.

'Oh, don't, Philip. It's nothing, really.'

'Well, clearly it is something. It's swollen, there, I can see, and it hurt when I took hold of it just then, didn't it? And your face is bruised, even if you have tried to hide it with your make-up.'

Annie arrived with the drinks on a tray. 'What has happened to your mother? Don't say it's nothing because clearly it isn't nothing.' Philip saw the two of them share a glance. 'Look, I can see you're not telling me something and by not telling me you're making me more angry and worried. Has someone done this to you, Jane? Because if someone has, I'm going to...' He broke off, aware that he was about to make an absurd threat.

There was a silence. All three of them became conscious that there were others in the pub, but fortunately they all seemed preoccupied with their own conversations. Philip turned back to the two of them.

'Jane, I know that someone has done this to your hand and face. We will not be leaving this pub until you have told me what happened.' After a very short pause, he continued: 'Annie, will you please tell your mother to tell me!'

'It's up to her if she wants to say anything,' Annie said.

'Say anything about what?' Philip demanded to know, feeling real concern.

'It's up to you as well, Annie,' Jane said, staring at her.

Philip saw the look they exchanged. 'Listen, I know you want to tell me, both of you. You wouldn't be here otherwise, and neither would I, obviously, so I think it's about time we stopped mucking about and you both told me what's been going on.'

Philip sat in silence as Jane told him that Bill had come back from Paris last night and had been abusive. They had had a row and he had hit her and then she had caught her hand in the front door as he tried to slam it shut when he stormed out and she had been trying to stop him so she could say what she wanted to say. It had been an accident, she insisted, totally unconvincingly. Philip seethed. He hated this man he had never met. He pictured a man with a permanently smug expression on his face. He imagined an odious, complacent, bullying, opinionated, arrogant idiot – and then he stopped himself, knowing he was being irrational because he was jealous. He was turning someone he really knew nothing about into some sort of monster.

'Is this the first time something like this has happened, Jane?' he asked, wanting the answer to be no.

'Yes. Well, it's the first time he has struck me on the face. There have been other times when...'

'When what, Jane?'

She hesitated, and looked at Annie.

'Go on, Mum. Tell him.'

'There have been plenty of times, but, well, it's happened more often recently. He deliberately smashed a vase. He has thrown his supper on the floor and hurled his glass of wine at the fridge door before storming out, leaving me to clear up. And he once knocked me when I was taking something out of the oven so that I burnt my arm. He said it was an accident, but it wasn't. Bastard.'

'Why has he behaved like this? How can he do this to you?' Philip was outraged.

'I accused him of treating the house like a hotel and I told him I wasn't his servant. He said he was the one who paid for everything. When I told him I knew full well he was sleeping around, he flew into a rage, and shouted, "Nobody could blame me, for Christ's sake!" I know he isn't faithful. I wouldn't be surprised if he was screwing someone in Paris a few days ago. That's what we were rowing about when he hit me across the face.'

'You said he punched you, Mum,' Annie said.

'I don't know what he did.' Jane was aware there were others in the pub and was trying hard to check her crying. Philip felt an overwhelming desire to protect her.

'I shouldn't be bothering you with this,' Jane said, reaching in her bag for some tissues. 'We're supposed to be having a nice lunch. Hold me, Philip. Please.' He did not need another invitation. He smelt her fragrance and felt how vulnerable she was and how small. Some of her tears fell onto his sleeve. He touched them and then tasted them and found himself deliberately misquoting: "*I have almost forgot the taste of tears*," he said. She half-recognised the allusion and turned her face up to stare into his eyes.

Jane chose the moment to add: 'He has also been abusive to Annie. Annie, tell him.'

Philip immediately started to dread what he knew Annie would say.

'Tell him, Annie.'

Annie looked around her and saw that the pub had become busier.

'Let's get out of here first,' she said. Without finishing their drinks, they got up and walked out, turning right and then right again through the blue gates into the grounds of Trinity. They walked in near silence, Jane holding Philip's arm, and Annie close beside her mother. They passed a huge, fragrant bed of lavender before finding themselves in a small patch of woodland, and they all saw a tree with a circular bench around its entire circumference. All three of them sought the shade the tree was providing.

'Go on, Annie. Tell him,' Jane said.

'I can't, Mum. You tell him.' Annie got up, moving back into the midday heat, and walked away, looking back to reassure her mother she really wanted her to tell Philip.

'It started after she got divorced two years ago. Bill was very solicitous about her welfare; I saw it often enough and was grateful at first. She often came round for meals and sleepovers and often it was because Bill had invited her, not me. He even worked from home on occasions so that he could look after her. Not that he's worked from home when I've needed any TLC,' Jane added bitterly.

Philip was anticipating what was coming next.

'And then,' Jane continued, her hands clasped tight on her lap, 'apparently he started getting all touchy-feely, putting his hand on her arm, wrapping his arms around her shoulders, holding her. She hated it but didn't want to seem ungrateful. She told me she hated the smell of his breath, the smell of his shower gel and his aftershave. It made her want to retch. And then... and then one day he had made her a coffee. They were both standing at the island in the kitchen. And he moved towards her and the next thing she knew he was kissing her. She swears she had given him no encouragement. She swears to God, she swears on my life. She says that she shoved him away and asked him what the hell he thought he was doing. He said he was comforting her. He said he knew she liked him. She told him he was her mother's husband. "So what?" he said. "We can both have a good time without saying anything to your mother." She couldn't believe what he was saying. She said he'd smiled and moved towards her, and then she spat in his face and rushed to the bathroom. What a bastard.

'She says he hasn't tried anything on since, but whenever she's at our house – and she won't come if she knows he's going to be in – he looks at her in a sleazy way and… and when he knows only she can see him, he… he touches himself and smiles at her. She hates him. We both hate him.'

Jane was shaking with fear and loathing.

Philip saw his daughter, heading back their way, tearful, head bowed. He went to her. He held her and she accepted his embrace, head still bowed. 'Oh, Annie, this is just so terrible. I can't bear to see you like this. This can't go on.' He turned to look at Jane. 'Jane, why don't you move out? Why do you put up with this?'

'What can I do? I can't throw him out; it's his house. And there's nowhere else I can go. And it's exactly the same for Annie. We can't report him to the police because he would deny everything and it would be our word against his. We're trapped. Oh, God. Do you know, I sometimes wish he'd have an accident and disappear from our lives.'

'I could very happily kill him,' Annie said.

'Don't say that,' Jane said. 'You don't mean that, Annie. That's not the solution, is it?'

'It would be if I could get away with it!'

They all froze and looked at each other, though nobody spoke until Jane broke the silence: 'Imagine that,' she said. 'Just imagine that.'

Philip had released Annie and was standing there in shock. Shock at what he had heard from both Jane and Annie, but also shocked that he was genuinely thinking he would be prepared to lose everything he had to make Jane and Annie happy. He cared more about them than about himself. He wanted them both to love him. What better way to earn their love than to save them from Bill? At that moment he felt he could kill him. He'd be prepared to play that role if that was what the script demanded. But what about his other family? How could they possibly understand or forgive him? They needn't know. They needn't find out. Nobody need find out. The deed could be done and he could escape undetected. Hundreds of crimes are never solved. Hundreds of murders. He thought about some acquaintances of his and Laura's neighbours. Young married couple, both accountants, apparently. Walking holiday. Fatal accident – the husband slipping and falling. But was it an accident? Nobody else there. Only one person really knew. He remembered reading somewhere that PD James suggested the best way to get away with bumping someone off was to go for a walk at Beachy Head and get too close to the edge and then give a little shove. It could be done.

He started to smile. He was looking at himself standing in Trinity College gardens with his daughter, his own flesh and blood, and the woman he believed he had loved for forty years and was seriously considering committing a murder. This was the Philip whose life had been completely unremarkable, whose story until the last week had been so pedestrian that nobody would ever want to read it. He saw the other characters in this new story: the beautiful wife being brutally beaten; the daughter suffering in silence; the repulsive man, abusing the two women and making their lives intolerable. And, yes, a man who would sacrifice his life to save the woman he loved. The tragic hero.

'I'll do it,' he said. The words somehow had just come out.

'Do what?' Jane asked, confusion and anxiety causing her to stop wringing her hands.

'I'll get rid of Bill. He will be removed from your lives forever.'

He closed his eyes, inhaled deeply and held his breath before slowly exhaling. The women didn't seek clarification or tell him he was being stupid. They simply looked at each other.

When he opened his eyes again, he was looking far away, determined and resolved, with a single-mindedness that would brook no contradiction. His eyes returned to Jane, but he didn't see the excitement in her eyes.

'Oh, Philip, don't be absurd. You are being ridiculous. It's a crazy idea. What on earth makes you think you're going to get involved in something so certain to lead to disaster, for all of us? I made my bed. I have to lie in it.'

Philip immediately looked at her and couldn't avoid picturing Bill in Jane's bed. 'Yes, you did make it and you have to lie in it, but you don't have to lie with him.'

'He hasn't shared my bed for months.' She looked at him. 'Nobody has.' He knew she was silently challenging him to share her thoughts, but he was already there and it was excruciating. He walked away from them, staring at his shoes, fists clenched. Jane followed him, leaving Annie on the bench, lighting a cigarette. She took his arm and turned him round to face her.

'Look,' she said, 'I know we can't go back to last Friday before we met in Worcester, and I don't want to, anyway. But can't we both, can't all three of us, just be happy that we have found each other again, and gradually and patiently and sensibly work out a way to deal with our new situations?'

'How can I be patient and gradual and sensible when I now know about Annie and when I know about him and when I still love you? Christ, Jane. You should have told me back then instead of keeping it a secret. For forty years! It's unbelievable. I wish with all my heart we could just go back to that summer. We could have made it work. I'd have done anything for you; you must have known that. We could have found a way.'

'Don't, Philip. Can't you see that I've had this conversation with myself thousands of times? I now know I got it wrong and that things could have been so different, but at the time it seemed the only way. And I have lived with it all this time. And I believed I was going to die regretting leaving you and never having the chance to tell you this. But something, some power brought us together last Saturday and what was going to remain unknown and unsaid forever has now been said. I'm sorry. I'm so sorry.'

She held him tight. He looked over her shoulder at Annie, his child. Living proof. The most miraculous result of something they had once had that was beautiful and which had been, even if only very briefly, so perfect. *It's such a mess and it hurts so much*, he thought, but he knew that he couldn't change what had happened in the past, and he wanted desperately to hold on to what he had newly found, and nobody was going to stop him.

'You can't go back to him,' he said.

'I have to. I'm going to leave him, but I just can't do it yet. I have to work out the practicalities. I hate him and I will leave him, but part of me knows this won't be enough. Leaving him won't mean he isn't still a threat to Annie, our beautiful daughter, Philip.'

'No, you can't just leave him, that's right. You can't let him get away with hitting you and abusing you, and you can't let him get away with what he has done to Annie. And I can't either. He needs to be punished. I despise him, Jane. I will not let him get away with treating you as he has, and I will not allow him to treat my daughter in the way he has. If he were here now I'd tear him apart, limb by limb.' He was taking short, shallow breaths, exhaling loudly through his nose.

Annie had joined them, pulled hard on her cigarette and inhaled deeply. Philip remembered when he had been a smoker for a short time. He knew how unpleasant he found it now and wondered how Jane had ever been prepared to kiss him. He remembered how sweet she had tasted and he was briefly taken back to the Ponte Vecchio and how she had smelt of Charlie. He smiled at the fact that he could not only remember the name of the perfume she used but could also recapture its scent. He felt an overwhelming sense of regret that his life, their lives, had turned out how they had. But he knew he was incredibly lucky to have a wife whom he loved and two wonderful sons. His story might be unremarkable, but it was a happy one, one he realised he should be so grateful for. But he felt that in the last week his conventional life had become remarkable, worth reading about even. And he knew that it was on the verge of becoming so dramatic that he couldn't help but smile at the role he'd been cast in. No longer a Rosencrantz or Guildenstern, a Guildenstern or Rosencrantz, but the Prince himself. He'd played the part often enough in class. *"'Bloody bawdy villain. Remorseless, treacherous, lecherous, kindless villain.'" Yes! I bloody well am Prince Hamlet, and was meant to be.* But he was not going to delay. *'The readiness is all' and I'm ready,* he thought.

'Philip, where are you? What are you thinking? Don't disappear like that. Stay here with us, please,' Jane pleaded, her face lined with concern.

'Oh, don't worry, Jane. I'm with you. I'm with you both, all the way. All the way to London. I am going to confront him. He will say I have no right to interfere in his relationship with his wife, but I have every right, in fact I have a duty, to tell him that if *ever* he treats my daughter again with the filthy disrespect and contempt that he has shown before I will personally see to it that he will pay a heavy price. *I will do such things…* he'll get the message all right.'

'Philip, no,' Jane said. 'You can't just walk into his home, our home, and dictate terms to my husband. He'd just laugh at you and tell you to piss off. And we don't need a knight in shining armour coming in on a white charger. We are perfectly capable you know. I can deal with him in my own way.'

'Jane, I'm not saying the two of you are poor defenceless women, for heaven's sake. I know you better than that. You can't have changed that much from the person I knew forty years ago. And I'm sure Annie is just as tough. But he needs to know that someone else is also on his case. He needs to know he needs to think twice before he abuses you or Annie again. He needs to know that you are leaving him and that he can't stop you, and I want to be there when you tell him. And I'll give him an ultimatum. I'll give him a warning. I know you are capable of dealing with this on your own, but I want to help you. It's my responsibility; it's my role.'

'What makes you think you have the power to do any of this? He'll just laugh, honestly. He'll laugh in your face.'

'He won't have the last laugh, I can assure you. Do you want things just to carry on as they are? Is that the future you want? Being trapped in a wretched marriage with a man who has obviously no respect for you? Living in fear? You have plenty of years ahead of you, plenty of time left. You have a chance to be happy again. To be free. To wake up in the morning looking forward to the day rather than dreading being with him or simply being alone. I will look after you, Jane. I can make you smile again. We can be together with our daughter. We have a chance.'

'Oh, Philip! We can't be together. You are married. You have a life in Worcester.'

'I can have a life with you and Annie, too.'

'No, you can't. You can't be with Laura and with me. I don't want to share you.'

Philip suddenly felt dizzy. What was he saying? What was he doing, standing in an Oxford college garden with his new daughter and a girlfriend he had once known, deceiving his wife and seriously considering going to a man's house to—

He broke away from the two of them. He needed space. He couldn't think straight when he could feel Jane so close to him, when he could smell her, when he was remembering her kisses, when he was remembering the rhododendron, the jasmine, the blanket, the tree and the moonlight. When he could see his daughter. He walked further away and they didn't follow.

I have two options, he thought: *catch the train back to Worcester and wipe the last week from my life; or catch the train to London with Jane and Annie and confront Bill.* He decided that the first option was impossible: he simply couldn't decide not to see Jane and Annie again. Life would be unbearable knowing that he was deliberately choosing not to see people he loved. And he knew they didn't want him to unknow what he had just discovered. And Jane's kisses. They made him feel alive, hot and cold at the same time. Each time they had kissed he had wanted to break the spell but also yearned for more. He knew she wanted him. He wanted her. They had still not enjoyed what he had planned for the last night of *Macbeth*. He would go to London, whether or not they protested, and confront Bill. He would tell him plainly that he knew what he had done and warn him that if he ever mistreated his daughter or her mother again he would go straight to the police. Yes, his daughter and her mother. This gave him every right. He was protecting his own, his loved ones.

He turned round to see that Annie and Jane had nearly caught up with him. Before they could say anything, he said, 'Please let me speak and don't interrupt. Annie, you are my daughter, and Jane, you are my daughter's mother. I have to do whatever I can to protect you. What sort of father would I be if I just stood by and allowed this to happen? So, I am going to go back to London with you. When your husband comes back, Jane, I will be there. I'll stay calm, I promise, but I will tell him who I am and why I am in his house and what I know about his behaviour towards both of you. I will tell him that if he ever abuses either of you again I shall go straight to the police. Don't worry. I am not a violent person and haven't hit anyone since I accidentally punched a friend at school when we were shadow boxing in the changing rooms after games one afternoon and I misjudged the distance between my fist and his nose. I shall not touch Bill, and anyway, he might be much bigger than me and I am a complete physical coward. I shall tell him straight, though, and I shall then leave your house and catch the next train home.'

'And then what? Will you then just disappear?' Jane asked, a hint of desperation in her voice.

'Of course I'm not going to disappear. I couldn't bear not to see you again. But I don't know what the solution is. We must be patient and see what we can work out. There's no rush. We have already waited forty years. I don't want to ruin things. We will find a way. I will find a way.' He paused and looked at them both. 'God, this is hard,' he said, and he didn't quite believe the situation he found himself in. 'Oh, Jane, I wish we were on the Ponte Vecchio and starting all over again.' He closed his eyes and briefly escaped in time. He woke up when he felt her arms around him. 'If we could go back, what would you change?'

'Don't, Philip. You're just making it hurt more.'

'Would you have ended it if you hadn't got pregnant?'

'No, of course not, but... oh, I don't know. How can I possibly know now what I would have done then? I did love you, you know. I had the most wonderful summer, too. You do believe that, don't you? I'll never forget it. I've never forgotten it. I still have photographs – and not just the one you saw last Sunday. There's one of you on the cliffs in Jersey that Jessica took, I think. You're looking at me. I think it was about a week after… after I opened up the blinds. I think I was very lucky that someone could look at me with such complete devotion. I have looked at that photo over the years. Lots of times in the last few years.'

Annie coughed theatrically. 'I'll buzz off, shall I, and leave you two to reminisce?'

'You're the living proof, Annie, of my love for your mother. Just imagine…' But he stopped himself, and stared into the distance, focussing on nothing he could see.

'I thought the plan today was to meet for lunch,' Jane said, reaching up her sleeve and bringing out a tissue. 'Shall we go back to The White Horse? Where would you like to go, Philip?'

'Let's walk up St Giles. There's a nice place on the left, just past St John's. I'm not sure I have much of an appetite, but you two can eat and I'll just look at you both. Do you know, I've taught so many texts over the years that explore the subject of memory, and how it's selective and how it distorts things and how it is multi-sensory, and here I am and it's real. Do you know the Hardy Emma poems?'

Both Annie and Jane shook their heads. 'Well, they're beautiful poems written shortly after his wife, Emma, died unexpectedly. They hadn't actually been getting on very well, but after she died, he made himself remember the best times, and the vividness of his memories is one of the things that make the poems so beautiful and so moving. In one of them, I can't remember which, he pictures her on horseback on the Cornish coast: *"The woman riding high above / With bright hair flapping free, / The woman whom I loved so, / And who loyally loved me."* He realised he wasn't quite managing to convey his thoughts or feelings clearly. 'Anyway, you should read them, the Emma poems. I love them. And…' He paused. 'Sorry, I'm getting sentimental. You two are seriously to blame. But memories have so much power. It's all your fault, you realise. I promise not to cry into my lunch.'

Annie took his arm, her step confident and determined. 'Where's this place, then? I'm hungry,' she said.

When they arrived, they were briskly but courteously shown to a table by a young waitress whose almost black hair was scraped back tightly off her face. When she returned shortly after with the menus, Philip was surprised to see that she had braces on her teeth, but she wasn't at all self-conscious about them and they didn't stop her smiling warmly at them after telling them about the day's specials.

Philip smiled when Jane ordered exactly what he predicted she would – the crab salad. But none of them ate heartily, all three of them subdued and emotionally exhausted. None of them wanted a pudding, even though he would normally have found the New York cheesecake completely irresistible. Annie did most of the talking, at his behest, trying to describe forty years in forty minutes. When she described a part of her life that was not happy, and there had been plenty, he could only wonder how different things might have been for her if he had been there to comfort her and to guide her and simply to love her. He felt her pain and unhappiness as though they were his own – as indeed in some ways they were. He couldn't really make up for lost time, but he could look after her from now on. Starting with confronting Bill.

Jane paid, reminding Philip that most times they had been out to eat in their summer together he had paid. He thought she was probably right but couldn't quite work out from where he had acquired the money. He also recalled buying her a bracelet as a present, and as soon as he'd bought it he realised he didn't like it because it looked cheap, chiefly because it was, but he couldn't afford anything else. He thought he remembered that it had been silver with some kind of pale blue flower attached to the chain. He had considered not actually giving it to her but had decided to in the end. He thought he remembered seeing a brief flash of disappointment on her face when she opened the little box, and he remembered how he had felt inadequate because of his poor taste.

Annie had checked train times on her phone and suggested to her mother that they make their way to the station.

'I'm coming, too. Don't try to stop me,' Philip insisted.

'I don't think you should. Why won't you let me handle this in my own way? You don't know Bill. We both really appreciate what you've said you'll do, Philip, but it makes me nervous. I just can't imagine it will achieve anything. It might even make it worse for Annie and me. This is all happening too quickly.'

Philip stopped her saying any more. 'What would you do if you were me? Just stand aside? Look, I swear I will not do anything silly. I am simply going to tell him it stops now for good or else. Right, let's go. Annie, you lead the way.'

Philip spent much of the train journey telling them about his other family, telling Annie about the half-brothers she had never met, had not even known about a week ago, and telling Jane about Laura, his wife of over thirty years. His mind went back to Hardy: *The woman who I love so, / And who loyally loves me.* He shared with Jane the irony that the Celia Johnson character in *Brief Encounter* was also called Laura. And he remembered that Laura's husband in the film, called Fred, he thought, had such a moving and beautifully understated line at the end of the film, when he turned to her and said, *You've been a long way away. Thank you for coming back to me.* He knew, even as he was travelling with Jane and Annie to confront Bill, that he would return to Laura. He was a long way away from her now, because time creates distance, and he was forty years away, in a time before he had even met her. He had to go to London, but he would return to where he belonged, in Worcester, to Laura who he knew would be waiting. Perhaps his life wasn't so unremarkable, after all. He felt confused but also incredibly lucky. The last week had taught him to appreciate both what he had once had and what he had now. He would do his duty in London and return to Worcester and tell Laura everything. She would understand and would welcome Annie into their larger family and learn to accept that he had once had something precious with Jane, but it was something different from what he had with her and would always have. He started to feel optimistic that everything could be resolved in time, that act five could end happily.

When they arrived at Paddington, Annie announced that she didn't want to be there when Philip confronted Bill. She did not want a discussion about it and didn't want to prolong the pain of leaving her father. In Philip's imagination she hugged him tight, told him she needed him, kissed him on the cheek and then walked off in the direction of the underground. Then she turned back: 'Love you, Mum. Love you, Dad. Love you both.' In reality, she had hugged her mother, touched his arm and said, 'Bye, Mum. Bye, Philip,' and hurried away.

Philip and Jane caught a taxi from Paddington and were soon back at her house. He hadn't seen her for forty years and now, in the space of less than a week, he had twice been in her home. 'I'll put the kettle on,' he said, forgetting the special tap, as Jane headed up the stairs.

'No, don't, Philip; I don't want any tea. Come with me.'

He followed her up the stairs, apprehensive about what he thought she was doing. She led him into her bedroom and closed the door behind them.

'I want to say sorry that our summer ended as it did. I want us to enjoy now what we missed then. If you don't want to, just say. I won't be offended or hurt, just very disappointed that you won't allow me to show you how I felt then and what I am feeling now.' Philip stared at her; he felt as though he had forgotten his lines. She moved towards him and reached up to kiss him. Her lips were just as they had been back then. He was taken back to Florence and also to the gardens where they had performed *Macbeth*. He could not bear the guilty pleasure and broke away.

'I can't do this, Jane. I just can't.'

'You can, but maybe you don't want to,' she said, goading him. 'It's just this once. We had unfinished business. It's just you and me. Nobody else is here. Nobody else need know. Don't you want to? You said you'd always love me and would always do anything I wanted. I want you now. Nobody has wanted me for so long. Do you still want me, Philip? *"Nor time nor place / Did then adhere and yet you would make both. They have made themselves."* She kissed him again, and he felt himself giving in. She had once had so much control over him and forty years had not taken away any of her power. Philip knew she sensed he was falling. She looked at him, her eyes taking hold of him so that he couldn't get away, promising him anything he wanted, then she broke away and walked into her bathroom.

Philip heard the shower being turned on. He didn't know what he was going to do and couldn't move from the spot. He knew he *should* go downstairs. He sat down on the bed and held his head in his hands, pressing his fingertips hard into his skull. What was he doing? How could he refuse such an invitation? *"Tis one thing to be tempted, Escalus; another thing to fall."* But this wouldn't be a fall. This was meant to be. Nobody was being forced to do something they didn't want to do. He would never have this chance again. Nobody else would know. And it was 1977.

He got up and walked into the bathroom. Her clothes were on the floor and he saw her through the steamed-up glass. He closed his eyes and saw her in their hotel room, the special surprise, both of them giddy with success and excitement after the last performance, him properly prepared this time. He saw himself take off his shoes and socks, and then the rest of his clothes and walk to the shower. He saw himself open the door. She was standing facing him, her hands by her side. He saw what he had glimpsed in the field under the oak. He walked in and closed the door. She moved towards him and held him close, their bodies gently welded together. He let the warm water cascade down his head and back. He did not want to move ever again. He wanted the two of them to be this close forever, two lovers in Pompeii preserved in this moment of absolute intimacy.

'Are you coming in or not?' she called.

He opened his eyes. He felt numb and terrified. At first he couldn't speak, but from somewhere deep inside he found a voice: 'I can't Jane. I just can't.' He saw her stop moving and stand absolutely still behind the glass. There was a pause and he could hear only the flow of water.

He stumbled back into the bedroom, his mind a jumble, tangled with desire and memory and guilt and confusion. *I'm sixty, not nineteen. This is not the last night. That was forty years ago. This isn't the last night I had planned for us that we didn't have. This is happening now. I don't have the protection, the overnight bag with your present, the bottle of Charlie. We are not going to spend the night together, and we are not going to wake up alongside each other. We are not going to clean our teeth together. We are not showering together. It is now not then.*

He looks up. She is standing in front of him, wrapped in a towel. He sees not a towel but her blanket. He sees the rhododendron bush, he smells the jasmine, he sees himself lying down, arms stretched above his head. He feels her hand, he tastes her tongue, and he sees the towering oak tree, the drunken car and the million stars.

'Can't or won't?' she asks, and he is back in her bedroom.

He looks into her eyes and makes himself say it: 'I can't, Jane. I won't.'

'Where's the spirit of adventure you used to have?' And he is instantly back in her Mini, on the way back from David's; swopping places. He remembers the rabbit and the hedgehog. The gear stick. Hitching her dress. He fights to push the memories away and finds some strength from somewhere.

'You are not Jane Thomas, aged nineteen. You are Jane King, aged sixty. Yes, I have loved you since I first saw you on the boat and somewhere in my heart I still love you. I have spent most of the last week back in 1977 and I have loved being there, Jane. But it isn't 1977. We moved on and we can't go back. Except in our memory and imagination.'

Neither of them speaks. He hears the slow drip, drip of the shower next door.

'It's half-past six,' she says, not looking at him, her voice suddenly flat and colourless. 'I think I'd like that cup of tea now, please.'

Philip left the room, not daring to look back. He knew that even now if he looked at her he would go back in, would never leave the room and there they both would be when Bill returned. He had promised he would stay in control and not do anything silly. He was settled, resolved. He noticed the hot tap again and put some tea leaves in the white china pot and sat down. Soon Jane emerged. She walked over to him, ready to speak. She noticed how his shirt collar was sticking up and straightened him out. He was taken back to the *Twelfth Night* rehearsal and he saw her again in the beautiful crisp white blouse, her collar settling with effortless perfection. He thought briefly about telling her what he was remembering but immediately knew it was too late. It was irrelevant. It was over; again.

She moved away a little. 'He could walk in at any time now. I will tell him who you are and why you are here. You will say what you said you would and then you will leave quietly. Leave all the rest to me.' She paused and moved towards him again, very close to him. He didn't move from the chair. 'Philip, please kiss me one last time?'

He knew he should say no, but he didn't want to refuse her this last wish. He stood up and they kissed, and behind eyes closed tight he suddenly saw her in a coffin, grey, her lips nearly white, her eyes shut forever so that she could never look at him again. The vision shocked him so much that he broke away. Bizarrely, he started to remember lines from Keats's 'Ode on a Grecian Urn': *Bold Lover, never, never canst thou kiss… For ever wilt thou love, and she be fair.* He hated the contrast – the urn's lovers would always be panting in ecstatic anticipation of their kiss and would forever be young, but he and Jane would never kiss again. *Never, never, never, never, never.* He thought back to their coffee in Worcester the previous Saturday. He wondered what he would be doing now if he hadn't met her on the Green. He asked himself if he wished he'd gone straight home after his encounter with James and not wandered around the stalls on the Green. He knew with unshakeable certainty he was pleased he had spotted her. The mother of his child. He closed his eyes to try to escape just for a moment the impossible situation they would have to face.

He had followed her without thinking to the sink, and he watched her as she used the tap to add the boiling water to the leaves in the teapot. He knew she was deliberately avoiding looking at him. Nevertheless, she started to speak: 'You have another family and I know you love them very much. I would like to meet them, to meet Laura. In time. And if we are careful and patient we can be friends. We share a daughter. All is not lost. There can be a future.'

He did not know how much she believed what she was saying, but he had little faith in the scenario she was starting to imagine. He just felt that the two worlds couldn't be brought together. He wasn't sure he wanted the two to collide. He tried to imagine a future with Annie but at that moment he simply didn't have the energy.

'Yes or no, Philip?' Jane asked.

'Yes or no what?'

'Would you like a cup of tea?'

The question seemed unutterably banal. He started to feel an overwhelming sense of exhaustion and misery.

'Oh, I don't know. No thank you. OK, yes, yes please. Sorry.'

'Don't be. I understand.'

They looked at each other and saw each other's desperate unhappiness. He said: 'Jane, whatever happens, now or in the future, I want you to know—'

They both heard the front door opening. He saw both power and fear in her eyes and felt his resolve stiffen as he sat himself down, determined to stay calm. Bill walked into the kitchen, and Philip thought he looked exactly as he had anticipated. Expensive suit which looked cheap on him, supercilious expression on his face. He was carrying a bouquet of flowers, absurdly large and grotesquely extravagant.

'I'm back, Jane. These are for you. I wanted to say sorry for...' Philip heard not contrition but arrogance in his voice. When Bill dropped the flowers on the work surface, Philip knew he loathed the oaf. He noticed Philip sitting at the table. He looked at Jane and then back at Philip.

'Hello, I'm Bill. And you are?'

Philip got to his feet and stood tall and straight. 'I'm Philip. I'm an old friend of Jane's.'

'Right. Hi. Nice to meet you. Jane, have you offered him a drink?'

'Philip and I were just about to have tea. But we can have a glass of wine if that's what you'd like.'

'There's a nice Barolo on the rack. Shall we have that? In fact, let me do it.'

'No, Bill, I can manage. You sit down.'

Philip could feel the tension in the air, the power struggle behind the superficially polite exchange of words between them. He could see in Jane's eyes her fear and her contempt for this man. He also knew already that Bill didn't like him being in the house, that he had been alone in it with Jane.

'So, how far back do you two go, then?' Bill asked, whipping off his suit jacket, throwing it over the back of a chair and sitting down on another and spreading his legs with the brash confidence that Philip knew Jane would find repulsive.

'Quite a way,' Philip said, feeling empowered by how long they had known each other. 'I first saw Jane when... well, let's say we first met when we were eighteen, in Jersey. We were both involved in drama – school plays and amateur dramatics.'

Jane interrupted. 'Bill, here's your wine. Philip, this one's yours, and please sit down again. Let's all sit down, shall we?' Jane joined the two of them at the table. Bill took a giant slurp, and the shape his mouth formed as he drank disgusted Philip; he saw an oily, ugly fish. There was a silence, broken by Bill.

'How come I'm feeling there's something slightly odd going on here? Why are you here, Philip?'

'Bill, just listen, please.' Jane took a small sip of wine and cleared her throat. 'I'll come straight to the point. Philip is Annie's father.'

Philip was shocked at the abruptness with which Jane had made the declaration and saw that Bill was taken completely by surprise and noticed how a look of fear flickered across his face before he quickly resumed his default expression of smirking superiority.

'Really? And you've decided to put in an appearance now, have you?' His aggressive tone was unmistakable.

'I'd have appeared a lot earlier if I'd known about Annie,' Philip said, looking at Jane to reassure her that he was not chastising her and neither was he losing his cool.

'So, you've just found out now that you've had a daughter for thirty-nine years?'

'I found out a few days ago, yes, that I have a forty-year-old daughter.' Philip could see that Bill didn't appreciate the correction and was irritated by Philip's calm manner.

'Oh, right. So you mean you didn't know about her? How did you find out then, after all this time?'

Jane stepped in. 'Bill, there's a straightforward explanation. When I was in Worcester last weekend for the concert, I bumped into Philip. He lives there. Obviously we were both surprised and pleased to see each other again. We hadn't seen each other for over forty years. We had coffee together and a drink after the concert and I decided I would tell him what I should have told him all those years ago – that he is Annie's father. So I invited him to London while you were away earlier in the week and I also invited Annie here. And I told them both.'

Philip could see that Bill was becoming agitated. He could see Bill's mouth working, his hands squeezing his thighs – his growing discomfort, not because this interloper in his house had once been intimate with the woman who would later be his wife, but because he had no power in the conversation, because he was not in charge. Philip could see Bill asking himself why this bloke had to be in his house, drinking his expensive wine.

'Is that it, then?' Bill said. 'Is that why you're here or is there another reason? If there's no other reason, perhaps you'd like to finish your glass of wine and then pop off to Clapham to see your daughter.'

He remembered the blanket, the car and the moonlight. The 'now, now'. And he heard Jane quickly intervene: 'Bill, don't be like that. It's not Philip's fault that I kept a secret for forty years. He is welcome in my house because he is the father of my daughter.'

Philip knew she'd got it wrong and had just increased Bill's anger. She quickly added, 'Of course I want him to be my friend now that we have met again. I'd like to think he could even be your friend, too. And I want to be friends with his family. He has a wife and two sons.'

'Why the hell would I want to be his friend, Jane? And I don't actually want this bloke who left you in the lurch all those years ago to be in my house.'

'But you're being absurd. What's he done to you, for heaven's sake? And he didn't leave me in the lurch. He didn't know. And it was me who broke it off. I broke it off.' Philip was in the departures hall again, holding the book. He heard her saying, 'And it's something I've regretted ever since.'

Philip looked at Jane, eyes wide and mouth half open as he inhaled sharply. What was she doing, inflaming the situation? But she wasn't going to be stopped; he knew how determined and defiant she could be.

He remembered what she had written and he saw the pencil-shaded armpit. He felt her hands on his thighs and saw her pinafore dress. He heard her say: 'Yes, I've regretted it ever since because he loved me then and he loves me now and has never stopped loving me. He cares about me and is kind and gentle and he always puts me first. He's shown more kindness and consideration for me in the last week than you have shown in the last twenty years.'

Philip knew he loved her, had always loved her and would always love her. Bill was smouldering in his chair, looking at Jane with contempt on his face and violence in his eyes. But she would not be deterred. Nothing was going to stop her now, but Philip tried.

'Jane, please don't say any more. That's not what this is about. We agreed that I would say—'

But she interrupted him. 'Yes, we agreed that you would tell him that if he ever hit me again you would go to the police.'

Bill stood up to protest: 'I've never hit you.'

'You lying bastard. Yes, you have, and here's a bruise to prove it,' she said, pointing to her cheek. 'And you, you bastard, you have made advances on Annie, you pervert, you disgusting bastard.'

He looked at Jane in fury and with panic in his eyes. He looked at Philip and must have seen contempt for him written on his face. Philip stood still and breathed slowly. How could he stay calm in this situation?

'Get out of my house. I want you out of my house, now, do you understand?' He stared at Philip, the usual smirk on his face now distorted into an expression of fear and loathing and desperation.

Philip saw Venus on her scallop shell. He saw the Witches' breasts and the apples. He was holding her hand, so small, so smooth. Her hand. He felt it. He heard her say, 'Well, I want him *in* my house.' *Now, now.* 'And I want *you* out of it. I want someone in my house who treats me with respect, someone who cares about my feelings, not someone who is forever going on about meetings and deals and money and me, me, me, big bloody me. He has given me joy in the last week. We made love in our bed just before you came back, and it was beautiful. Not the revolting, the disgusting – all you ever cared about is yourself.'

He didn't know where he was. What was she saying? They hadn't made love, had they? Where was he? The blanket. *I haven't. Double, double gin and tonic.* He spluttered: 'Jane, look at the stars.' He turned to Bill. 'We did. We did. She loves me.' Philip saw fury in Bill's eyes. He knew Bill had no feelings for Jane, he knew that and he could see it for himself, but being cuckolded was different. He could see that Bill thought nobody would get away with humiliating him like that. He saw again the volcanic anger in Bill's eyes. On his face were hatred, despair and humiliation. And jealousy. *She loves me, not Bill. Has always loved me.* He strokes her ankles and hears the sea below. He feels her head on his stomach and then her lips on his. He sees Bill hurl his glass at Jane, the wine spattering her blouse and the glass smashing on the cupboard behind her. He sees Bill rush at her and grab her violently around the throat.

'You fucking bitch. Fucking witch. You ungrateful slag.' He hears these words spew from Bill's ugly mouth. He sees him shove her hard against the cupboard behind her, smashing her head. Jane's bulging eyes are pleading with Philip. He knows he must be as good as his word.

Philip hates violence, goes cold and shivers whenever he sees a violent scene in a TV drama, but this is different; at this moment he is someone else, in a different place and time, and he pulls a knife from the block and thrusts it into Bill's neck. For the briefest of moments he is happy that his action is an entirely reasonable way to deal with the situation; it is in the script. But then he is suddenly back in her kitchen, and blood is spurting everywhere, and Bill tries to grab Jane's blouse before slowly slumping to the ground, incredulity on his ugly, contorted face. He twitches for a few long seconds, and then is still, blood seeping out of his neck and his mouth.

There is a long silence as both Philip and Jane stare at the body at their feet. 'No. No, no, no, no. Christ, what have I…? I didn't mean to… it wasn't me, it was… I was back in… he was… Jane, why did you tell him – are you all right?'

She is standing over Bill's body, looking at the blood pooling around her feet. He has stopped moving, his face still, his eyes looking somewhere far in the distance for an explanation. Philip begins to shake uncontrollably. He thinks of Laura and his boys. He has just ruined their lives and they will never forgive him. He thinks about removing the knife from Bill's neck and plunging it into his own. But he can't move from the spot. Jane has sunk to the ground, eyes wild and breathing heavily. He wants to lower himself so he can slump beside her but he can't move. He notices how blood has drained from her face and she is as pale as Bill. He manages to crouch and takes her hand but it is cold and lifeless. Again. He sees how much blood is on the floor and knows there is too much to clear up. *Who would have thought the old bastard? A little water wouldn't be enough. Oceans wouldn't be enough.*

He looks at him again and sees the look in his eyes. But then he can't see anything clearly and the room swirls and he looks at his hands. *Where am I? What has happened to my beard? Where is it?* He wants to scream, but no sound comes out. He starts to shake. He sees Jane, crumpled, still not moving, Bill's blood trickling towards her skirt.

He knows he is shaking violently but everything is happening in slow motion and everything is now silent. He sees a rivulet of blood creeping along the grouting of the ceramic tiles.

Jane is staring up at him. He sees a face distorted into terrified and ghastly incredulity. Slowly her slack jaw starts to move and he hears her form some words: 'Philip, what have you done?' He looks at her and slowly, with nauseating clarity, it occurs to him that this is not what she had wanted. He stares at his hands and feels his heart thumping, each pulse a drum beating deep inside him and reverberating against his skull.

'It was my fault,' she says. 'I wanted to hurt him. I wanted to see him squirm.'

'No, Jane. I did it. And it was *his* fault.' He feels a new energy start to rise, slowly and irresistibly, from inside his stomach. 'He had you round the throat.' He looks at her. 'I had to save you.'

He fumbles in his pocket for his mobile. Hands shaking, but his focus sharp, he dials 999. He hears himself answer all the questions and feels his breathing become strangely subdued.

When 10 minutes later the police and ambulance arrive, within 30 seconds of each other, Philip has lifted Jane from her collapsed position on the floor and they are both sitting at the table. The knock on the door is loud but does not sound particularly urgent, and Philip calmly goes to let them in before they might feel the need to use force. He leads them through the hall, past the drooping white roses, into the kitchen. Bill is sprawled on the floor and blood has spread across more of the tiles and is seeping under the kitchen units. The knife is still in his neck, the entire blade buried.

'I did it. Me. It was me. I did it.' Philip intends to be calm and to explain what had happened but the words come tumbling out, unsolicited.

Immediately one of the two policemen leads Philip to a corner away from a rigidly motionless Jane, and stands opposite him, his back to the rest of the room.

'And what is your name, sir?'

'My name is Philip Robinson. The victim is Bill King. He is married to my friend, this lady. She is Jane King. He was hurting her and I grabbed one of the knives from that block over there and drove it into his neck.'

Philip looks up to see figures he presumes are paramedics have also arrived and some scene of the crime tape has already sectioned off the kitchen on the other side of the island. He looks at Jane who has still not moved and then back at the policeman who is staring at him, the expression on his face suggesting he is very wary of him. He feels compelled to relieve the policeman of his anxiety and confusion. 'I am not angry any more and I am not a danger to anyone else, I promise. I will stand here patiently until you take me away. I will answer any questions you have to ask.'

'What were you doing in this house, sir?' the policeman asks.

'I was here to confront Mr King. He had been abusing my friend and her daughter, my daughter, and I came to warn him that if he was violent or abusive again I would inform the police.' Very briefly, and despite feeling numb and exhausted, he considers the irony in his words. 'He lost his temper and started to attack Jane, grabbing her around the throat and he shoved her into those kitchen cabinets. I saw the block of knives, took one out and plunged it into the side of the neck.'

Philip hears one of the paramedics or the other policeman confirm over a walkie-talkie that the victim of the attack is dead. He stares, unbelieving, at his hands and his head spins as though he had just got up too suddenly. He thinks of the photograph on his mantelpiece of him and his wife and sons at the rooftop bar somewhere near St Paul's.

He looks at Jane. She has a ghostly expression on her face but looks startlingly beautiful. He tries to look inside her head. She looks at him searchingly. *What shall I tell them?* she is asking. He believes she is thinking that it was her words that had incensed Bill and provoked his attack, whereas Philip had kept his promise, had stayed perfectly calm right until he had come to her defence. Still looking at her, Philip slowly and scarcely perceptibly shakes his head. She should stay quiet. He intends to take full responsibility; she is an innocent victim.

Forensics have arrived – white suits, white slippers and flashing camera. *Just like in* Silent Witness, Philip thinks, and he remembers all the happy times when he has watched episodes of it at home with Laura. Suddenly he tries to calculate how many more seconds there still are before the lives of Laura, Tom and George will be irreversibly shattered.

He is given next to no warning and can't stop himself from vomiting explosively and copiously on the floor in front of him. He wants to wipe his mouth but he can't move his arms. Jane sees his discomfort and pulls a handkerchief from her skirt pocket. She moves towards him, quietly rejecting the policeman's insistence she stay away from him. She dabs his mouth clean, and his nose, and then gently wipes away the film of perspiration that has appeared under his eyes and on his forehead. He looks into her eyes and remembers them lit by candlelight at David's dining table and by the fire eater's flames in the Piazza della Signoria.

A female police officer has arrived and immediately introduces herself to Jane. As she is doing so, Philip is instructed to walk out of the house to the car that is waiting outside to take him to the police station. He has promised he will do exactly as he is told, and he keeps his word. He looks back at Jane and knows he has kept his promises to her, too: *I will do anything for you; and I will never stop loving you.* The police car is waiting directly alongside Jane's house, blocking the middle of the road, blue light flashing. Philip remembers the red light flashing at the entrance to the harbour. He thinks of Gatsby and the green light on Daisy's dock. He waits for the protective hand on his head as he gets into the car and he feels disappointed, cheated, when it doesn't come. *That's what they always do*, he thinks. *Why am I being denied the moment?* His head is throbbing and he fears he will be sick again. The car is dreadfully stuffy but he doesn't think it would be wise to ask if the heating could be turned down. As the car pulls away, he remembers Jane and Annie on the steps waving to him the last time he had left these premises, and he wonders if he will ever see either of them again.

26

OCTOBER 2018

WORCESTERSHIRE

'Thank you for coming,' he says. She doesn't say anything. He continues: 'I would understand it if you didn't come to visit me, you know.' Still nothing, and she can't look at him. 'I'm so sorry, Laura.'

'It's a bit late for apologies, isn't it.' A statement, not a question.

'Yes.'

She finally looks at him. They hold each other's glance briefly, and then her hand goes to her mouth as she shakes her head in incredulity and closes her eyes, frown lines deep across her brow.

'I just can't understand why you, how you—'

'I know. I can't either.'

Silence. It continues.

'How are the boys?'

'What do you think? They're both back at work full-time now. Tom has lost a lot of weight. George is coping a little better. You know – he's just put on the blinkers, determined to get on with life. How were they when they visited last week?'

'George just wanted to know exactly what had happened and how. He simply wanted to understand. But I don't understand it myself, so how can he? Tom was more quiet and a bit tearful. He found it hard to look me in the eye and—'

'Not surprising, is it.' A statement, not a question. They look at each other, Laura conscious that it's pointless being short with him but unable to avoid it, Philip aware that she has every reason to be much, much less civil than she is being. Laura continues: 'They will both survive. They're strong.' Philip knows that she is also strong and will also survive. She has always been strong – for the boys and for him. Now she will be strong for herself.

'You have had a long time to reflect, Philip. If I am ever to understand and perhaps one day accept what happened, you are going to have to explain it to me. I don't know if I will ever be able to forgive you for what you have done to the boys, but I may be able to forgive you for what you have done to me if I can understand what you were doing, and what you were thinking.'

He thinks about reaching for her hand but knows he has no right to do so. Instead he stares at it and then finds himself thinking of Jane's hand. He sees the ring on Laura's. Thirty-five years of happy marriage. A few months of excitement forty years ago and a week of madness forty years later. And he knows that it was madness. He has nearly committed adultery and he has killed a man. He looks at his own hands, already looking thinner, pale and weak. *What hands are these?* he thinks.

'I really do want to tell you, to explain. This is me now and it wasn't me then. God, it's so hard to explain. It was as if I had no control over what was happening and yet at the same time I was willing it to happen. I know that's contradictory, but that's how it was. It's almost as if I knew it was going to happen and I couldn't stop it, partly because I didn't want to.

'I was obsessed with Jane when we knew each other all those years ago. When she reappeared in the summer I thought I could turn real life into fiction. I wanted to be part of a different story. I wanted the excitement of turning my life into something dramatic, something remarkable. You don't read novels or see plays or see films about predictable, ordinary people, about people like me. Novels and plays are about risks and danger and madness and adultery and murder. Think of our friends and the people we know and which ones we talk about. We don't talk about the steady Eddies. We talk about people whose lives are disrupted or dangerous.' He suddenly thinks about Miller's play *A View from the Bridge*; they had seen together a production of the play in Birmingham a year or two ago. 'Yes, that's it,' he continues. 'We don't talk about or get excited about steady Eddies, but we do talk about Eddie Carbone, do you remember the play, because he's a man who loves his niece and is prepared to die because of it.'

She is looking at him, trying to understand. He tries again: 'Whom do you remember, Tess or Mercy Chant? Why is it called *The Great Gatsby*? Why do we read *Madame Bovary*, *The End of the Affair*?' He stops and looks at Laura, desperate to see that she understands, that he is making sense.

'So I'm not dramatic, not exciting enough? Is that it?' Laura asks.

'No, that's not it, Laura, I promise. It wasn't like that. I love you and George and Tom more than I can say. In the rational, cold light of day I am more thankful than I can say for our life together, for the last thirty-five years. I have been incredibly lucky. Our boys are wonderful and all three of you mean so much more to me than Jane, infinitely more, I swear, but something made me want to be… to play a new character just for once, and I couldn't stop myself. All the time I knew it would end in disaster, but I got into something and I couldn't get out. I thought I had. I said no to her. I thought I had escaped, but I hadn't. I hadn't got out. I didn't mean to… It was simply going to happen. You probably think I'm mad, but I'm not. I'm not mad now, but maybe I was for that week. I knew what was happening all along and I was able both to be part of the story and at the same time to observe it unfold. When I, when I picked up… when I stabbed him, I was watching myself do it as if I were on stage. And as I saw the knife in his neck my first thought was, *Yes, that's right, that's what it says in the script.* I had played the part as written. If I hadn't done it, the play wouldn't have worked; it would have just fizzled out. I wouldn't have been worthy of her love.' He stops when he sees Laura's eyes drop. He knows what she is thinking so quickly explains.

'Yes, I wanted to be worthy of her love. But that's because we were both back in 1977 again. Throughout that week we had both talked about that summer and how things might have been – if the next forty-one years had been different. There was, there was still – we had some unfinished business. And it would happen once, and once only, and would never happen again. But it didn't happen, I swear. It nearly did. But it didn't, I swear to you. But… but then it went wrong. My God, it went wrong.' He looks at her and sees what he thinks is not understanding but at least a willingness to try to understand.

'And Annie?' she says.

'Almost too unbelievable even for fiction. I don't know. She hasn't visited. I was protecting her, too, you know? I can't bear the thought of never seeing her again. She isn't Tom or George, of course she isn't. But she is my daughter and I think

I love her. Because it's not possible to feel anything else, is it? It's desperate knowing that I won't be able to play a part in her life for the next... for the next however many years – having already not played a part for the first forty.'

'She is your biological daughter. She means more to you than the boys. Do you know how much pain that causes me, Philip?' She is fighting back her anger and her tears, her pale skin blotchy, her nose red and starting to drip.

'That's not true, Laura. Please don't torture yourself with that thought. It's not true, I promise. I've only known Annie a couple of months. I've loved our boys for twenty-five years and will always love them.' He pauses. 'I love you, too,' he says, almost inaudibly, daring himself to say what he feels but fearing she will despise him for saying it. His throat is choked with pain. He can see her terrible distress as she struggles to process his words. 'It's fair to say that I've fouled up quite a few lives.' He looks at her, his mouth twitching as he tries desperately to hold back the tears stinging behind his eyes. 'I'm so very sorry, Laura.'

The bell sounds for the end of visiting time. He thinks she seems quite keen to leave, and, standing up, she takes a hanky from up her sleeve, wipes her nose and then replaces it.

'Will you come next week, do you think?'

'Yes, I'll be here.' She walks away and doesn't look back. His mind suddenly leaps and he sees Jane walking out of departures and not looking back. Forty-one years ago. A lifetime. Someone's lifetime, anyway.

Laura collects her belongings from the locker and makes her way back to the car park, knowing that her life can never be the same again. But the sky is still bright blue and completely cloudless and the warmth on her back as she walks towards the car allows her a brief moment of hope, though it quickly dissolves as she contemplates the lonely journey back to an empty house. She wants Philip to be with her so that he will do the driving and she can enjoy the scenery. Yes, she does want him with her, she thinks. She briefly stops in her tracks so that she can ask herself quite specifically if she really does want him with her. She stands quite still. And she decides she does. Yes, she really does. She knows she does. The realisation for just a moment lifts her spirits a little and she nods, swallows and then looks back over her shoulder before resuming her walk to the car. But then she remembers he won't be with her for several years.

When she arrives back home she is shocked that she can't remember any of the journey. She had not been conscious of any other vehicles, had not been aware of any of the music playing on Classic FM and doesn't know how the last hour has passed without her being aware of anything that happened on the road.

She had been thinking about Annie, replaying some of the thoughts she had had when she had first heard about what had happened. How could Annie be blamed for anything? Her part in all of this had been being conceived, being born and then living without a father all her life. None of this was her fault. She was to be pitied rather than condemned. She deserved her sympathy, not her opprobrium: no sooner had she gained a father whom she had not known for her entire life than he had disappeared in disgrace. Annie's existence was no reflection on Philip's relationship with her or Tom and George. As she remembered these reflections, she saw that she was being rational but she also knew that it would take more time still to be reconciled to them, to accept them, to be able to live with them from day to day. She had thought adjusting to the different circumstances would be equally difficult for the boys, but she had to admit now that they had been not only accepting of Annie's existence but keen to know her; Tom had even met up with her on one occasion.

She had also been thinking about Jane, again. When Philip had made the one phone call he had been allowed after his arrest, he had, she genuinely believed, told her the truth and not tried to hide or disguise anything. In her desperate state, she had instantly hated Jane, but not long after she had changed her mind when she saw that she couldn't hate someone she didn't know, no matter what she had done. In the days that followed she had tried to visualise Jane, had even googled her, but had been unable to find a photograph. She had worried that she must always have been second best, had always been the consolation prize. But she couldn't believe that all of the good times they had had together had been anything other than special for them both. She couldn't believe that he had been hiding his true feelings and only pretending to love her, simply making the most of what he had. Haunted though she was by that possibility, and how it would mean that most of her life had been a charade, herself the victim of an elaborate deception, in her heart she knew he had loved her; and loved her still. One week couldn't destroy thirty-five years. One week couldn't transform the man she loved into a different person even if it had turned him into someone who had committed a murder. He had been a different person for those five days, but they were now over and he was himself again, not the fallible fictional character, the tragic hero he thought he had wanted to be.

She had lain awake at nights trying to understand how Jane had exerted such control over him. How could someone from over forty years ago be so enthralling? She herself knew what it was like to yearn for lost youth, for the excitement of the past. She felt herself that their lives were less exhilarating than they had been, but that surely was what happened when you reached their age. She thought about whether she could ever be unfaithful. She knew she couldn't, but she had also thought that he couldn't be either. And he would surely have said the same. But he had been, almost. He had maintained ever since that dreadful phone call that what had happened in that week in August had in their minds been happening in 1977. She had at first completely dismissed his claim, accusing him of ridiculous and offensive nonsense. She had for a time despised him for his sophistry, despised him more for that than for the adultery he had nearly committed and the murder.

She kept returning to Jane, taking no note of what would have been familiar signposts and names as she continued her journey home. How could she have made Philip do it? How could someone make the mildest of men commit an act of brutal and clinical violence? Philip had claimed that when Bill had grabbed Jane around the throat he did what he knew he had to do to protect the person who in his mind at that moment was his nineteen-year-old girlfriend. The knives were on the work surface to help him defend her and he had used one. Laura was prepared to accept the possibility that at that time he had genuinely believed he had been nineteen again, but she couldn't believe that the Philip she knew could ever have been a nineteen-year-old capable of such an act. But then, quite suddenly, something clicked in her brain and she knew that somewhere in his over-active mind he had not only imagined he was playing the part of his nineteen-year-old self but also an infinitely more famous and dangerous role. She believed she would eventually be able to understand. And that realisation provided some comfort: more comfort than most of her friends and her siblings who had advised her to start to make a new life for herself, a life without Philip.

Such were her thoughts when the car arrived back in its space in front of their house.

She switches off the ignition and the sudden silence makes her realise where she is and the fact that she must have driven back in some sort of trance. Briefly, she wonders about how extraordinary the mind is, how she hadn't had an accident even though she had been 'miles away' all the way home. *The mind is so strange, so powerful,* she thinks: *it can make you completely oblivious of the reality of a situation. Yes, perhaps it can make you believe you are in an entirely different time and place. Yes, perhaps it really can make you think you are a character in a play.*

27

NOVEMBER 2018

WORCESTER

When Jane turns into the drive and parks in the space left vacant for her, she sees a fair-haired figure standing at the long window looking out at her. She has rehearsed many times what she is going to say but all of the preparation suddenly seems inadequate and she starts to feel the beginnings of panic. The woman is still staring at her. Jane asks herself if she is doing the right thing.

A few days after Laura had last seen Philip, Jane had visited him. Their exchange had been punctuated by long silences, as they tried to help each other understand.

'Why did you do it, Philip?'

'You know why I did it, Jane. I was protecting you. He had you by the throat. When you told him we had made love, he lost it. He was furious and grabbed you. How could I just stand by?' She looked at him and then down at her hands held tightly in her lap. 'I heard you say it, Jane. You said it was beautiful. You said you still love me and always have.' He willed her to look up to meet his challenge. He waited. She slowly lifted her head and stared hard at him, her face lined with pain and confusion. 'Why did you say those things, Jane? You may have wanted to torment him, but don't you understand that you also tormented me?' He knew she wanted to say something but needed to do it in her own time. He decided he would risk everything. 'You knew what you were doing, Jane. Why did you do it?'

Her eyes were red and the skin on her face had become heavy and dull. 'You used me, didn't you?' Philip said.

'Yes.' The admission seemed to soften the air between them, and he suddenly felt a surge of sympathy for her. He looked at her, trying to force her to look up so she could see he had already forgiven her.

'I hated Bill,' she said, 'and didn't want him in my life but I thought you would simply help me stand up to him. I didn't want you to kill him, Philip.'

She looked up and saw his face. She knew he deserved a fuller explanation. She had thought carefully for several days about what she would say, the act of preparing her words helping her to understand herself what had happened. She looked completely exhausted but knew the hardest part was only just starting.

'My life has not been a great success, Philip. My marriage was deeply unhappy. I should never have married him. I have reached the age of sixty and feel desperately unsatisfied. Life had promised so much. When I met you in Worcester, like you, I was taken back to when we were young. That was a time of such excitement and such promise. It was such a golden time. I was so often the centre of attention and loved it. Exploited it, I'm ashamed to say. Exploited you, I know. Tormented you, I know. It was exhilarating having that power. But I also loved you, Philip. As I have never loved anyone else.

'I just took for granted that a glorious future was laid out before me. Life was thrilling and the prospects were so good. But it all changed. It all changed so suddenly. And I never really blamed you, Philip. It was my own fault. And I marked time for the next forty years.' He wanted to hold her. He couldn't bear to see her so miserable. But he knew she had more to say.

'And then we met in Worcester. It was impossible not to be taken back and I wanted to experience that excitement again. I was shocked at the intensity of the desire. I wanted to relive those special weeks, the best days of my life, Philip, I swear to God. You hadn't changed. You seemed to worship me all over again. It means so much, to know that you are loved. To know that someone still finds you exciting. That life is urgent again. That blood still courses through your veins. That someone wants to kiss you. That someone desires you and wants to make love with you. You did want to, didn't you?' He said nothing but just looked at her and she knew it was true. She felt a sea breeze blowing gently. She knew that he understood.

He reached across the table, knowing he would give anything to hold her hand in his once more. But she hadn't finished.

'Don't, Philip. Everything I've said so far has been easy. Relatively easy, anyway.' She reached up her sleeve for her handkerchief. 'I feel ashamed about this, and I'm sorry, but yes, I did use you, Philip. I used you, simply because I could. I always could. God knows I didn't deserve your devotion when we were younger. But I loved having it. I loved having the power to inspire it. And I could tell when we met back in August that I still had it, that you were still devoted. And I exploited that power because I haven't had it for so long. That's the sad admission of someone who promised so much as a teenager but who went on to achieve so little. The happiest and most exciting months of my life were those I spent as a teenager with you.' They looked at each other and Philip felt himself surfing a wave of exhilaration.

'I didn't mean you to kill Bill. But I did use you, and I will admit this fully in court.'

'No, Jane. I shall take full responsibility. I wanted him to attack you so that I could show you I would do anything for you. I wanted to protect you. I have always wanted to protect you. When we hugged on the Ponte Vecchio and whenever I held your hand I just wanted to look after you.'

'But I could always look after myself.'

'I know, but that didn't stop me wanting to.'

Suddenly she found herself fighting back convulsive sobs.

The desire to reach for her hands was now almost overwhelming, but still he resisted. She placed her hands in prayer before her face and kissed her fingertips. She closed her eyes as if in preparation.

Her face almost contorted into tears. There was a pause before she continued, in barely more than a whisper. 'Things would have been different if we hadn't met, wouldn't they? I should never have married Bill, but it had been hard trying to make a career for myself with a dependent child and when I met him, after a number of failed relationships over a period of years, it seemed a good option. I was wrong. Having lots of money doesn't really help, you know?'

'But that doesn't mean you regret having Annie, does it?'

'No, Philip. Never. I love her with all my heart. But my life has largely been shaped in the way it has because of her existence. Everything could have been different.'

Philip imagined a beautiful blue butterfly settling on her head.

'Do you wish we hadn't made love on that night?'

She knew that it was now or never. 'No, Philip, I don't.' As she took a deep breath, she felt a surge of determination. 'But I had drunk too much. I think you knew that. We shouldn't have. *You* shouldn't have.'

Philip thought he was swallowing water from a fetid pond. He said, 'But you were as eager as I was, Jane.'

'Yes, I was, I wanted you so much, but you were supposed to have protection, and I was drunk, Philip.'

'Your hand. You took—'

'No, Philip. That's not how it happened.'

'It is, Jane. You wanted to, as well.'

'Yes, Philip, I did want to, because I loved you, but for once you took advantage of *my* love for *you* and I was not in full control and you knew that.'

'You said, "I want you. Now. Now."'

'No, Philip, I didn't. Those were *your* words.'

She had spoken. Something she had thought about for over forty years.

And so had he.

She looked as though her stomach had been emptied and she felt light-headed. She had reached the top of the cliff and the sea had come into view. She could feel the breeze and taste the salt air.

She looked at his crumpled form and his broken face. She thought he might never speak to her again. There was a long silence and he couldn't look at her.

But he knew that it was now the very last opportunity, and he was not going to miss it this time. 'I love you, Jane. I have loved you since I first saw you, and I will always love you. But from now it must only be in my memory and in my imagination. It's safer that way.' He lifted his head and looked at her, feeling there must be infinite sadness visible in his eyes and on his face and in every cell in his body, slumped as it was on the cold metal chair.

There was only one more thing he would ever say to her. He forced himself to face her and to look into her eyes: 'Jane, I'm so very sorry.'

He had said it.

'Philip, you are a good man. I loved you throughout our summer. I never experienced feelings like that again. Until last August.' Staring at him still, she said, 'You will always be in my heart.' They held each other's gaze. And then he looked away.

She looked again at her hands, twisted in her lap, and cleared her throat. 'I want to ask you something,' she said, shifting in her chair and not daring to look at him. He said nothing, so she looked up. 'I want to ask your permission to visit Laura.'

Silence. Neither of them heard the whispers and mumbles and metallic scrapings in the room. Neither of them was aware of the stale smells of the other inmates or the cosmetic pungency of their visitors. The silence continued. Until Jane added, 'I want to say sorry and to try to explain. And to tell her that we had two seasons in 1977 and that she has had the last thirty-five years and will have the future. I want to tell her that she never lost you.'

Silence again.

She continued: 'Unless you say no, Philip, I shall take your silence to mean yes.'

Silence again, broken by the harsh metallic indication that their last meeting was at an end.

She saw his limp white hands on the table in front of him and she gently placed hers on his. They were both completely still.

'Thank you, Philip. Goodbye.' She turned to go. He saw her departing, just as she had done after the *Twelfth Night* last-night party, just as she had done at the airport, and as he saw her recede into the distance, he said, 'I love you.' But not out loud.

Jane notices that the woman has moved from the window and has opened the front door. She quickly steals a look in the vanity mirror, picks up her bag from the passenger seat, and gets out of the car.

'Hello, Jane.'

'Hello, Laura. Thank you for allowing me to come.'

'Come in.'

Laura leads Jane into the sitting room and invites her to sit down on the sofa. Jane wants to look closely at the room, at the photos on the mantelpiece and on various pieces of furniture but she knows she has no right to, that it would be an invasion of Laura's privacy, so she sits stiffly on the edge of one of the sofa cushions, hands folded on her lap. She knows she needs to take the initiative, to start the conversation. She has requested the meeting, after all, not Laura, so she is surprised when Laura speaks.

'I know this must be very painful and difficult for you. I don't know if it will help in any way, but I want you to understand that I don't hate you and I don't blame you for anything that has happened. Philip made his own decisions, just as he always has, and we all have to live with them.' She pauses. Jane thinks she is going to continue, but when she doesn't she knows she has to speak.

'I realise that anything I say will be totally inadequate and nothing that has happened can be changed. But I want you to know how sorry, how very, very sorry I am about what happened. I feel deeply ashamed. Even now I can scarcely believe that I was capable of being so selfish. My pain and anguish must be as nothing compared with yours, and having to live with what happened is no more or less than I deserve.

But I am so sorry that you and your two sons also have to endure the consequences.'

Her speech sounds prepared but they look at each other and both know it is heartfelt. Laura has expected to hear such sentiments, but Jane knows she has not expressed what she really wants to say, that what really matters is hovering invisibly but insistently in the motes of dust hanging in a sharp sunbeam between them. She tries again: 'Laura, what Philip and I had for a few months when we were nineteen was precious and I have never forgotten it. I am not too embarrassed or ashamed to say that to you. It is simply a fact. But you have had his love for over thirty-five years and still have it. I don't think you ever lost it. What happened during those five days was madness. We were not ourselves. When we met by the cathedral on that August Saturday he was transported back to 1977 and he took me with him and we lost control. And… and there is Annie, of course, a living reminder.' She looks down at her hands. 'In that week he lived out a fantasy, a fiction, a fiction both of us were writing, reading and enacting, all at the same time. But it is over now. Philip and I will always have that summer. But I only have him now in my memory and imagination. You have him in reality. You have him as flesh and blood – not just the faded photographs I have of the two of us all those years ago.'

She stops. They look at each other. Jane feels drained and thinks she will never be able to move again. In her heart, Laura wants to believe what Jane has said. In her heart, she feels pity for this woman who is left with so much less than her. This woman whose only crime, she thinks, has been to have loved a man who has been married for thirty-five years to somebody else.

They sit together in silence for a short while. Jane gradually feels some strength returning to her body and knows it is time to leave. She stands up and moves slowly to look at the photo of Philip on the mantelpiece. He is with Laura and two young men, all four of them smiling, St Paul's in the background. She thinks briefly of the Duomo in Florence, of the Uffizi and the Piazza della Signoria. Of their meeting on the Ponte Vecchio. The photo looks recent, taken perhaps a year or two ago. She is perplexed by the young men's dark hair and olive complexion. Laura, who has also stood up and is now by her side, sees her surprise. Jane then dips into her handbag and brings out the photo she has brought to show Laura. Laura stares at it.

Jane thinks she needs to explain: 'That's the two of us playing—'

'Yes, I know. I've realised that. I didn't recognise him straight away, but I do now.' She lifts her photograph off the mantelpiece, pauses briefly to think, before saying, 'That's all of us last spring. Me and Philip with our boys. They're adopted, you know. He probably told you. A loving father and husband. That's so much more the man I know.'

It isn't intended to be, but it sounds like the last thing that should be said. Jane slowly nods and walks towards the front door, trying to process what she has just heard. Then she notices something on the short bookcase in the hall and she pauses for the slightest instant, imperceptibly to Laura. At the end of the top row, the last volume is protruding slightly more than its companions. It is an old paperback copy of John Fowles's *The Collector*. She remembers the airport. She remembers giving it to him. She can remember writing the words inside the cover. She remembers, too, the picture on the front – of a girl and a butterfly. *It could have been so different*, she thinks.

Laura opens the front door for her and Jane steps out and walks towards her car. Laura immediately closes the door and then goes back into the sitting room. Neither turns round.

ACKNOWLEDGEMENTS

I am grateful to the following people for reading a draft of the novel and for their helpful comments: Sarah, Sophie and Emmie Le Marchand; Jackie Sonsino; Lucy Walmsley; Sue Mason; and Rosemary and Peter Diamond. Special thanks to Cressida Downing who pointed out things I already knew but was trying hard to ignore and who made numerous other very instructive suggestions.